Straight

CHUCK TINGLE

Copyright © 2021 Chuck Tingle. Second Edition.

All rights reserved.

ISBN: 9798749499698

CONTENTS

CHAPTER 1   1

CHAPTER 2   Pg 20

CHAPTER 3   Pg 35

CHAPTER 4   Pg 56

CHAPTER 5   Pg 67

CHAPTER 6   Pg 81

CHAPTER 7   Pg 98

This community is stronger together than any one of us could ever know. Thank you for being a part of that strength.

- Chuck Tingle

1

I remember a time when I didn't care about anniversaries. My exes would give me hell when the inevitable days arrived and, of course, I'd feel bad about letting these important milestones slip my mind. This forgetfulness had nothing to do with my love for them or the state of our relationship, just a simple expression of my own disdain for the calendar year.

It all just seemed silly, so needlessly traditional, especially given the fact that my relationships were rarely traditional to begin with. Sure, we've made it one rotation around the sun together and the time that we've shared is deeply important, but why does this cosmic distance even matter? This oval route isn't the only path we're traveling on in a constantly expanding universe, so it's not like we've truly arrived in the same location we started from.

Everything is moving in ways too complex for most folks to even begin comprehending, myself included, and yet we're all completely obsessed with these measurements of time, buying each other flowers after every successful solar trip.

I hated anniversaries before it was cool, long before the events of April 7th.

Of course, not everything can be a perfect unit of time when the grand design of the universe is in the driver's seat. According to scientists, Saturation Day will fall approximately two days earlier every year, and so far they've been right.

This is our third rodeo, and the evening of April 3rd is our new target.

How the hell they managed to calculate such a thing is beyond me. I've tried my best to follow along with the various news reports, but at this point all the stress leading up to the big event is too overwhelming to logically consider much of anything.

Fortunately, I've got a whole two-hour car ride into the middle of nowhere with Hazel by my side, and she's the smartest person I've ever met. Especially when it comes to this kind of thing.

I realize suddenly that I've been standing here for a good ten minutes, just staring at the wall of my apartment with a duffle bag in my hand. I let out a long breath and abruptly realize my entire frame has been clenched up.

It's understandable given the stress I'm under, but I'm also worried this gradually blooming anxiety might be something more. What if it's really a crazed, uncontrollable rage?

It's absurd, I know, but trauma has a way of making you second guess even the most fundamental parts of yourself.

STRAIGHT

I shake my head, pushing these thoughts away and trying my best to refocus. I can't go staring at my wall again for the next hour—my friends will be downstairs any minute.

Kicking into gear, I begin my final supply check, making my way around the place to confirm all necessary items have been gathered. My phone charger is no longer in the wall near my bedside, which means it's safely stowed away in my bag. My special new ultra-sensitive toothpaste is missing from its holder, ready to treat this mouth that's been grinding away endlessly in my sleep.

Eventually, I arrive in the kitchen, my eyes falling upon the butcher's block as I stop in my tracks. I'd been toying with the idea of packing a knife, which still seems utterly absurd, but it's the new state of the world we live in. The whole point of heading out into the desert like this is so I won't need to stab anyone, but the phrase *better safe than sorry* has rarely been more applicable.

Finally, I walk over and pull the largest blade from this wooden block. I hesitate a moment, considering the emotional weight of this choice, then push it back in. I don't need a knife, I tell myself, and if I *do* need it then maybe it's better to not have one handy.

I glance over the low wall that divides my kitchen and living room, gazing at the ground in a very specific spot in front of the television. The floor is wood, and it's currently bone dry, but in my mind's eye I can still see the bloom of dark crimson making its way across this surface. There was so much liquid it became oddly reflective, a red mirror that no minor scrape or slash could ever create.

No, you need a *lot* of blood to see yourself gazing

back.

It's all cleaned up now, though. Sorting out the apartment and putting things back in working order was quite the process, but by then the whole world was working together hand in hand. It was genuinely inspiring how people came together directly following the first Saturation Day, but I suppose they didn't really have much of a choice.

I blink rapidly, pulling myself back from this second trance. There I go again, lost in thought on the one afternoon I should be laser focused.

"Okay, time to go," I say aloud to myself, as though this vocalization will somehow force the phrase to permeate my skull.

I pull out my phone and check the time. They'll be pulling up any second.

Without another moment's hesitation. I open the door of my apartment and step out into the hall, turning around and locking it behind me.

I burn this task into my mind so I'm not worrying about it later, triple checking that I've secured the simple lock as well as the deadbolt.

The last thing I do is, of course, the strangest. Out of my duffle bag I pull a folded piece of paper and a roll of tape, then diligently get to work as I affix this handwritten message to the door. I make sure my sign sits directly at eye level as I tape down every corner.

I'm not inside, it reads in bold, handwritten marker. *On vacation.*

Since this is only the third year of dealing with crazed cisgender straights, it's hard to tell if something like my sign will work. The first Saturation Day was utter chaos,

STRAIGHT

but a successful vaccination program made year two a lot more manageable, at least by comparison. The true mental capacity of *the overwhelmed* is still difficult to pin down, but it appears they have a childlike understanding of reality mixed in under all that destructive rage. If someone's primitive brain tells them to storm down the hall and kick open the door of their bisexual neighbor, maybe this little sign could stop them.

It's worth a shot, at least. While I certainly wouldn't have to pay for the repairs, I'd rather my place wasn't completely trashed when I got back.

I turn around and gasp at the unexpected figure standing next to me.

Fortunately, my fear is quickly dispelled when I see who it is, immediately recognizing the sweet older woman who lives on this floor. She's got a small rolling suitcase next to her and is holding a clear plastic container packed full of freshly baked cookies that smell absolutely incredible.

"Margot," I blurt. "I didn't see you there."

"Looks like we're both hitting the road tonight," she observes, nodding toward my duffle bag. "You stay safe out there."

"I will," I reply warmly. "I'm headed into the desert with some friends. Nobody around for miles."

Margot narrows her eyes. "You don't want to pay for one of those safe zones? West Hollywood?"

I shake my head. "Too many people. Last year was a bit of a…" I hesitate before using the word *clusterfuck*, quickly shifting gears. "A bit of a mess."

Margot nods, then turns and starts gradually making her way down the hall toward our building's main elevator. I follow along next to the sweet old woman, taking my time and keeping her company. They say symptoms of The Blank Space will start revealing themselves up to twelve hours before transitioning into a full on rage, and so far Margot seems perfectly normal. She's her usual smiling self, a little quiet and dawdling, but just as kind as ever.

"Eighty percent of people got the vaccine," she informs me.

"But it doesn't work on everyone," I remind her, "and unfortunately there's a lot of folks lying about it."

"That's true," she admits as we reach the elevators. She pushes the call button. "You know, *I* didn't get the vaccine."

I shoot her a confused glance. As far as I know, Margot is an intelligent, liberal-minded woman with a gay son and should, therefore, be first in line to get the shot.

She notices the look on my face and lets out a bit of light, tittering laughter. "Oh, not because I didn't *want* it. I'm too old, they won't let me."

I nod along, suddenly reminded of yet another demographic I'll have to watch out for this evening. Fortunately, Margot's a little slow to cause much harm.

"So what are you gonna do tonight?" I question.

"Grant's got his place all set up for me," she explains as the elevator arrives and the two of us step on. "He has a basement with no windows to crawl out of and a big thick door. I feel like a werewolf!"

I raise my eyebrows, nodding along as I press the button for the first floor and we begin our descent. I'm trying not to react to the thoughts that are suddenly flooding through my head, the idea of this frail woman screeching and hissing as she attempts to scale the walls of her self-imposed underground prison. She'll do anything she can to strangle her own son tonight, but I don't think that's going to happen.

At least, if she can get there before nightfall. Fortunately, there's plenty of time to spare.

"Well, it's really nice to know you're taking the right precautions," I offer in return.

Margot reaches out and takes my hand in hers, giving me a firm squeeze. "I'm so sorry," she sighs, a powerful weight in her voice that immediately changes the atmosphere within this tiny lift.

There's a quiver in her tone as these three simple words slip from her lips, and while I'd love to tell her that it's all okay, I simply can't bring myself to do it. I want to say it's not her fault, that nobody could've seen Saturation Day coming and that she didn't ask for her brain to be overwhelmed by homicidal rage, but I remain silent.

I like to think of myself as a relatively balanced person, which is why it's so difficult for me to admit the resentment I still harbor. I'd love to push it all away, to forgive the rest of the world for what they've put us through, but right now I'm in no position to do so.

The best I can do is change the subject.

"Those cookies smell good," I tell her. "Are those for your son?"

Margot nods. "Oh yes, I was baking them all morning," she informs me. "Fresh from the oven. You want one?"

The tiny woman takes back her hand and then slowly peels up the blue transparent lid of her plastic container, allowing the potent scent of these sugary baked goods to flood my senses with homesick nostalgia.

"Oh no, I'm fine," I reply, waving her away.

This denial is nothing but instinctual politeness, spoken well before I've had a chance to actually consider how much I'd enjoy one of these delicious morsels.

"You sure?" Margot continues, opening the lid a little more and holding the container under my nose.

"Okay, okay," I finally give in, accepting her offer with a laugh. "Thank you."

I reach in and select one of the golden brown chocolate chip cookies, then let out a startled yelp as pain erupts through my hand. I pull back in shock, glancing down to see that a single point of brilliant red is starting to form on the pad of my thumb.

"Are you alright?" my elderly neighbor questions, deeply concerned.

"Something pricked me," I blurt, holding my fingers together in an attempt to stop the bleeding.

I try again, this time gentler with my grip as I extract the dangerous dessert. I hold the cookie up to my face and look it over, my eyes widening as I realize an assortment of sewing needles, thumb tacks, and a single quarter have been baked into its flakey crust.

Returning my gaze to the rest of the cookies, I notice now these treats all contain a variety of household knick-knacks. One of the sugary disks has an entire ink pen speared through it, while another encloses collapsed, skeletal remains of a severely dehydrated goldfish.

"You should try it," Margot offers.

"I'll save this for the drive," I reply with a nod and

the most convincing smile I can muster.

The woman is staring at me with frightening intensity now, frozen in place with wide eyes and an enormous, unnatural smile plastered across her face. The two of us linger like this in the tiny elevator, this moment stretching on and on as I struggle to appear natural.

I'm well aware of tonight's schedule, fully expecting straight people to start acting a little off during the hours that lead to Saturation Day's grand arrival. Baking a few household items into your chocolate chip cookies is par for the course.

It suddenly dawns on me, however, that the science is still out. There's plenty of room for error.

Maybe Saturation Day has already started, and the second I step off this elevator I'll be surrounded by utter chaos.

I take a deep breath and let it out, collecting my thoughts. I remind myself that most people got the vaccine already and it's not going to be like year one. I remind myself that every year we're going to be a little more prepared, and things will be handled with a little more grace.

Still, the anxiety continues to build within. It's not the larger implication of tonight that has me tense, it's the threat standing right here in the lift. It's Margot's eerie, disconnected smile.

She's too frail and old to hurt me, but that's not my concern. I'm worried I'll have to hurt *her*.

The blood stain in the middle of my apartment living room suddenly flashes through my mind once again, bathing me in horrific memories of the very first Saturation

Day. I see it all, remember what I had to do to save my own life.

The elevator doors open and Margot's expression changes, faltering slightly as she shakes her head from side to side.

"I'm sorry," the woman gushes. "I forgot what we were talking about for a second there."

"It's fine," I reply.

The two of us stroll into the lobby of our apartment complex, where Margot's son is waiting for her. They hug warmly before Margot hands over her bag and the cookies. She shuffles out to the car as Grant turns to greet me.

"There's needles in the cookies," I quietly inform him.

"What?" Grant blurts, my statement not quite registering.

"Don't eat the cookies," I explain, scrunching my face awkwardly before nodding toward the plastic container in his hands.

Grant lifts the lid, peering inside cautiously, then grimacing when he sees the dead fish. "Oh God, she cooked Betty," he sighs.

"Stay safe tonight," I offer.

"You too." The man notices my bags. "Skipping town?"

"Headed out to Joshua Tree with some friends," I share. "We'll keep the lights low and play board games. There's nobody around for miles."

"All it takes is one overwhelmed to start making a bunch of racket," Grant replies, concerned about my plan.

"You didn't wanna just hunker down in your place with a movie and a handgun?"

I shake my head. "I can't do the *fight back* thing anymore. We're gonna take our chances and avoid confrontation entirely."

My words strike a chord with Grant, who glances back at his mother. The woman is sitting shotgun in his car, gazing out the window and waiting for her son to join her. It's hard to tell if her expression is genuine, or if she's starting to feel overwhelmed again.

"I hear you," Grant finally replies with a nod. "Stay safe, Happy Desaturation Day."

He pats my shoulder and heads for the door, leaving me to stand in the apartment lobby and wait for my friends alone.

You can tell a lot about someone based on what they call this yearly phenomenon. Desaturation Day was the original name, one of several monikers that just happened to stick when the whole world was lost in a state of deep mourning. This reference was a nod to the rainbow flag, which remains a symbol of pride in the LGBTQIA+ community. When all the cisgender straights lost their collective shit on April 7th, the queer death toll was catastrophic, not to mention all the hetero folks who died when their targets fought back.

Of course, the easiest symbol for news reports and magazines to use was a grayscale rainbow flag, often when actual footage of the carnage wouldn't be appropriate.

Eventually, the title Desaturation Day stuck; the day our rainbow flag lost its color.

This name didn't last long, however, revised as the

community started rebuilding our lives. If there's one thing the queer community is, it's resilient.

Soon enough, the language around this tragic event began to evolve. It was asked that desaturated rainbow flags be retired so the vibrant colors could return.

We'd mourned, and now it was time to refocus.

While Desaturation Day is still the *official* term, those of us who believe we can move past all this trauma and carve out a brighter future prefer Saturation Day.

Once a year, the colors of the rainbow flag will shine with even more brilliance. Because they have to.

Two quick beeps of a car horn announce my friends' arrival and pull me from my trance. I gaze across the lobby and through our massive front windows to see my crew idling at the curb, waving excitedly.

"Isaac, what the hell are you doing?" Nora calls over from the back seat. "Is your straight half turning into a zombie already?"

As a bi guy, I'm not entirely comfortable with the implication that I'm half of *anything,* but when it's a bit of razzing from one of my closest friends, I let it slide. Nora's the type who can't help herself when it comes to inappropriate jokes.

I grab my duffle bag and head out into the California sunshine, making my way around Jason's car as the trunk is popped.

"I was actually just thinking about how you should go fuck yourself," I retort with a smile.

I shut the trunk and continue around the other side, sliding into the backseat next to Nora and giving her a warm hug. The whole gang greets me lovingly, offering gestures of affection as we pull onto the road and begin our journey toward the desert.

There are four of us piled into the vehicle, a ragtag assortment of friends from all parts of the queer spectrum. Of course, we've got plenty of straight friends, too, but tonight we're staying as far away from them as possible. Even the ones who've proudly received their yearly vaccine—blasting injection images across social media with the requisite pride flags attached—can't be trusted. There's no guarantee whatever's causing this hasn't shifted and mutated in some way over the last three hundred and sixty three days. A shot that subdued all symptoms last year could easily be rendered ineffective this time around.

On what is only the third annual Saturation Day, there's simply not enough information to work with.

Or maybe everything will be fine. Maybe the whole world will join as one and put this thing to bed for good, relegating Saturation Day to a bizarre phenomenon taught in history books. Things were slightly better last year, after all, and there's no reason for that to change.

I notice now that Jason, the driver, is gazing at me intensely in the rearview mirror. "You okay, buddy?"

"Yeah, it's just... today is a lot," I admit.

Jason is a large, muscular man with pale skin and reddish hair that stays shaggy on top before wrapping its way around his face in an impressive beard. He's an old friend whose severity I still haven't gotten used to.

Jason nods, accepting my response, but I can't help thinking there's a little more than friendly concern there.

I'm a bisexual man and I've dated plenty of women. *Mostly* women, actually, and while this used to make someone like Jason uncomfortable, on Saturation Day it makes them utterly terrified.

Hazel, who's sitting in the passenger seat, notices the subtext of our exchange and quickly steps in. "Hey Jason," she offers. "Not cool."

"What?" he retorts defensively. "What do you mean?"

"She means quit being a dick!" Nora adds from the back.

Jason hesitates for a beat, then softens. "I'm sorry, I'm sorry," he apologizes. Jason reaches back over his shoulder, his eyes still on the road but his palm open to me behind him.

I grab my friend's hand and give him a squeeze, letting him know that I'm not upset, at least not enough to make it a thing right now. This is a difficult time for everyone.

I glance over at Hazel, noting that she's also feeling uneasy regarding her place here. I suppose the two of us have a lot in common in that respect, which is probably why we get along so well.

Hazel is a lesbian trans woman and is deeply in love with Nora. She sports long blond hair that contrasts against her dark skin, and dresses with a distinctly conservative look that takes formality to the edge of appropriateness. Hazel is always styled with her own unique brand of boardroom chic, like she's headed to some gloriously fashionable business meeting. It's a combination I admire.

After the first Saturation Day, most hateful detractors were silenced when relationships like Hazel and

STRAIGHT

Nora's proved, once and for all, that the trans experience is a valid and integral part of the queer community. Trans people, both straight and gay, were unaffected by homicidal rage, and TERFs were kicked even deeper into the dumpster where they belong.

Unfortunately, whenever Saturation Day looms near there's still an unspoken sense of pushback from within the queer community. A deep subconscious fear that, like bisexuals, trans folks might unexpectedly find themselves overwhelmed.

It's disgusting, and our once large social group has grown smaller because of it.

I don't miss them.

Suffice to say, there's a lot of energy moving back and forth within this vehicle. We're all dear, dear friends, but you could cut the tension with a knife.

"I can't take this anymore," Nora finally announces, leaning all the way forward across the car's central console and turning on the radio. "Can we *please* just have a fun little Joshua Tree getaway this weekend and forget all the bullshit?"

A wave of upbeat pop music immediately floods through the car speakers, the consistent rhythm feeling invasive and out of place but also providing a much needed distraction. Nobody says a thing, just lets the song wash over us as the streets of Los Angeles roll past.

Nora is small in stature, but she doesn't mind taking up space. She's freckly, with jet black hair and intricate tattoos cascading across either arm. I absolutely love her, and it's moments like this that are precisely why.

I gaze through the window, observing a city on the

verge of complete lockdown. Windows are getting boarded up as businesses close early, settling in for the evening. The majority of the world's population will rest easy tonight, straight and safe. So long as they've been vaccinated and taken the necessary precautions, there shouldn't be much of a problem.

Still, it's not a cakewalk. Plenty of clear-thinking straight people were attacked while trying to protect their loved ones during last year's Saturation Day, although reports of this kind of thing are still a little fuzzy.

Some of them are likely queer folks hoping to remain in the closet.

The pop song continues to roll, a blissfully happy soundtrack to the apocalypse, and before long I actually find myself nodding along. I've heard this one before, and by the time the chorus comes back around for the second pass I'm humming the hook, a smile slowly creeping its way across my face.

Suddenly, just as quickly as it arrived, the music disappears.

Jason has turned it off, plunging us back into silence as he stares through the windshield with a gravely serious look on his face.

I can tell Nora wants to protest, but even *she* knows to hold back.

"I get that you all wanna have a good time this weekend," our friend begins, "but maybe we should reassess what this trip is about."

"Oh my god!" Nora finally blurts. "I *knew* you were gonna do this."

Jason hesitates. "Do you realize how many people

nine percent of the global population is? Do you realize how many people *sixty percent* of the queer community is?"

He asks these questions as though we haven't been bombarded with statistics from the previous two Saturation Days, but we have. For a long time, it's all that we *ever* heard.

They used to say one out of every ten people was queer, but if there's one thing Saturation Day taught the world it's that these figures are way off. Turns out there's a lot more of us out here than we'd originally thought.

While some embraced this global outing, there were plenty of right-wing conservatives claiming they were the exception to the rule, that they weren't the target of some rage zombie mob *because they were gay,* but because there'd been a simple cosmic error.

Maybe it was the devil testing the faith of their followers.

Nobody believes these charlatans, but they've got a point about the exact numbers being hard to pin down. Even the world's greatest statisticians don't really know.

Thankfully, we've got something better. We've got Hazel.

"Hey, how's Australia doing?" I ask. "Hasn't Saturation Day already started over there? Shouldn't we already know if this year's vaccine is working?"

This is a technical question, and while I've posed it to the entire car, Hazel knows I'm really just directing it to her.

"Actually, The Blank Space is so large that when Earth passes by its field of influence, the shift will occur at almost exactly the same time across the globe," Hazel explains, turning around in her seat to face me. "The full effect will hit California at eight fifteen this evening, and it lasts a little under twenty-one hours. In Sydney, it's going to start around one in the afternoon."

"And they're sending out probes, right?" I question, hoping to spark conversation within the vehicle's awkward silence *and* genuinely fascinated.

"Yes, there's an unmanned probe called Sokos 12 that'll scan The Blank Space just after nightfall, but they've been sending them out for months," Hazel explains. "That's part of the program I was working on last fall."

"What did they find?" I continue. "It's like a black hole, right?"

Hazel shakes her head. "It's literally nothing; a void. A black hole effects the energy and matter around it, but The Blank Space is just... empty. It's a completely new scientific phenomenon. Clearly, it's affecting all the cisgender straight people, so there must be some kind of energy field, but we don't understand what kind of energy it is, or even have a great method of detecting it. We only know how far out this field of influence extends because of where people on Hermes 3 and 4 were effected."

"I can't even begin to understand how all that is calculated," I offer in return.

"The calculations are... vague, but it's something," Hazel replies. "Saturation Day seems to be shortening, though. In a hundred and forty years they expect we'll be completely out of range. We got lucky. The Blank Space could've just as easily been drifting closer."

"Luck isn't the word I'd use," Jason interjects.

"Don't be jealous that my girlfriend is a super

genius," Nora offers.

I suddenly notice a group of armed soldiers standing on the corner as we slow down for a red light. They're wearing the usual United States military fatigues, clad in green camouflage from head to toe, but they're also sporting a colorful rainbow patch on their shoulder.

"Oh my god," I blurt, my eyes going wide. "The gay militia!"

I heard on the news that cities across America were getting help from this new marine branch, but I hadn't yet seen it for myself. While some communities, like Palm Springs, put their entire budget toward this kind of protection, Los Angeles was opting for a minimal, but visible, presence.

"Those guys are so fucked," Jason observes. "If something goes wrong, this whole city is coming for them."

Nora is undeterred by this observation, rolling down her window and leaning out to greet the soldiers. "Heeeeyyy!" she cries, waving excitedly as she playfully stretches the word into a sing-song cadence.

The men and women in uniform smile and wave back as the flow of traffic continues. Cars honk when they drive by, showing their support.

We settle in as the big city starts gradually giving way to a suburban landscape. As our vehicle pulls up onto the freeway, Jason reaches out and turns on the radio.

The two of us exchange glances in the rearview mirror again, only this time his gaze has softened.

Music fills the air as we cruise toward the desert, trapped somewhere between a weekend vacation and the end of the world.

2

"You *know* we're gonna stop at Bobcat's Saloon," Nora states loudly, her voice cascading through the vehicle with utter confidence while her body remains sprawled across the back seat in a comfortable slump.

I turn my head away from the glorious scenery, glancing back at my friend and then to Jason in the front. Since leaving the sprawl of Los Angeles, their conflicting views of this trip have become even more apparent.

Meanwhile, Hazel and I just stay out of it, taking in the desert views with an air of somber reflection. The landscape of rolling yellow hills and seemingly endless desert flora is something to behold, and it's hard to be depressed as it passes by us in a steady stream. There's something magical about this place, that's for sure.

Even in the face of potential Armageddon, the natural world is still breathtaking. Everyone could skin each other alive and the desert would still be here. Hell, it'd probably be better off.

STRAIGHT

Jason stays quiet, allowing Nora's assertion to hang in the air for a while. He waits so long to reply that I'm not sure he ever will, but eventually he opens his mouth to speak.

Before the words have a chance to spill forth, however, Hazel interrupts with a shocked cry of her own.

"Oh my fucking God!" she blurts, pointing out the window as we crest a rolling hillside.

We all see it now, a towering inferno spilling forth from a vehicle on the side of the road. The car is absolutely torched, orange flames billowing out on either side as a plume of black smoke fills the air. A tow truck sits next to the wreckage, YUCCA VALLEY TOWING painted in bright orange letters across the side.

As we draw closer, three figures can be seen standing near the frightening scene. They don't seem all that worried about the blaze, and they're staring directly at our car as it approaches.

Also, they're completely nude.

Jason slows a bit and rolls down his window. "Do you need help?" he calls over.

On the left, a couple is smiling wide, huge grins plastered across their faces as they wave like some kind of animatronic greeters from a funhouse ride through hell. Standing to the right is the tow truck driver, naked save for the blue and orange Yucca Valley Towing hat on his head.

"Nope!" the tow truck driver calls out, his smile unchanging.

Jason nods, then glances over at the rest of us before speeding up and continuing on our way.

"You sure you wanna stop at the saloon?" he asks.

I turn to watch as the flaming car disappears behind us. The naked couple act as though we're still there, waving to the empty place where we'd spoken to them.

"Yeah, let's stop and get a drink," Nora continues.

Jason lets out an audible laugh. "Are you fucking kidding me?"

"Folks are getting a little strange already," I offer, finally chiming in. "The lady in my apartment building tried to feed me chocolate chip and sewing needle cookies before I left."

"Yeah, but she wasn't *trying* to hurt you," Nora counters. "She was just confused, like those people back there."

I glance over at Hazel for confirmation. "Technically, she's right," my friend nods. "A percentage of the straight population are going to start behaving unusually, but they're not aggressive until the big shift happens around eight. Right now, they're probably more dangerous to themselves than to us."

"So we've got plenty of time!" Nora continues. "That's like five hours!"

Hazel nods reluctantly.

"I thought the plan was to stay quiet and play board games," Jason continues. "Now we're stopping at some bar for drinks?"

Nora scoffs loudly. *"Some bar?* I'm talking about Bobcat's. Have we taken a trip to J Tree and not gone to Bobcat's? Has that *ever* happened?"

Jason reluctantly cracks a smile, some memory of a previous drunken night at the saloon no doubt creeping its way back into his mind. He glances over at Hazel.

"Are you sure it's safe?" he questions, deathly serious.

Hazel immediately shakes her head. "Oh no, I never said it was *safe*, I'm just stating the facts. We'll want a ten-minute buffer before we lock ourselves in for the night, but until then we're not going to run into anyone who is fully overwhelmed."

"Are you *sure?*" Jason presses.

Now it's my turn to interject. "She's not sure, okay?" I blurt. "None of us are sure of anything right now. The point is, we can't just live in fear. We need to find a balance. I could've just stared at an imaginary blood stain in my apartment today, but instead I came out here to be with my friends. Is that safer? I have no idea. But here we are."

The car falls into silence again as the radio continues to play. While the music had once felt like a beacon of positivity, it now just seems kind of strange.

"Listen, when I threw my bag in the back I noticed there were no groceries, so we'll need something to eat," I offer. "We should go to Bobcat's and order a drink, then get some takeout for later."

"I figured we'd just hit the market in town," Jason replies. "In and out."

"Market's a half hour past Bobcat's," I remind him. "Everything closes early tonight. You're not gonna make it."

"Fuck," Jason blurts.

"How's your gas?" I continue.

Jason glances down.

"Fuck," he repeats.

I can't help but laugh at how woefully unprepared

we are, and yet the fact I can find *any* humor in all this is a potently optimistic sign. Deep down, I know that tonight's gonna be fine. Since the first Saturation Day, things have only gotten better, and out here in the desert there's simply not enough people to create the massive shrieking hordes that are seared into my memory.

I don't want to be stupid and pretend there's nothing dangerous about this evening, but I'm sick of all the doom and gloom.

Balance, I remind myself,

"We've got enough fuel to get to the rental, right?" I question.

Jason nods. "Yeah, it's fine. We'll just fill up before we head home when things open back up tomorrow."

"Here's the plan," I say, taking charge of the situation. "We stop at Bobcat's Saloon for *one drink*. We order some food to-go while we still can. We head to the cabin and get settled in *extra early*. We play Boggle and I kick everyone's ass. We sleep. We wake up and stay quiet until…" I trail off and let Hazel fill in the technical details.

"Approximately three in the afternoon tomorrow," she offers.

"Then we celebrate," I finish.

Jason sighs and finally caves. "Yeah, I could use a drink. *One* drink."

It's not long until Bobcat's Saloon comes into view, a restaurant and bar that resembles the quintessential old west watering hole. This place is rustic and weatherworn, wood and stone stacked high with a large sign above the door in burnt western lettering. Massive, pale green agave plants line the building, tracing along the walls until they reach the double-door entrance.

Beyond this structure is Pioneertown, a small collection of businesses who've dedicated themselves to a unified old west theme. They gather to create their own nineteenth century main street in the middle of nowhere. There's a shooting gallery and a variety of souvenir shops, as well as a haunting gallows platform that sits in the middle of the avenue.

The whole place is deserted.

The four of us climb out of Jason's car and head for the saloon, the desert heat ruthlessly beating down from above.

That's one positive thing about nightfall, things cool down.

"Are you sure they're open?" Jason rightfully questions.

With no sign of life to be found, I have my doubts, but we push through and immediately find ourselves greeted by a huddle of men at the bar.

There are four of them. The guys are all gruff and unshaven, two with dark, tousled hair and the others sporting a cowboy hat and a trucker's cap. Their clothes are dirty and tattered, and one t-shirt features the face of a country singer I've never heard of.

The potent juxtaposition of our groups causes both sides to freeze in our tracks, awkwardly assessing one another.

"Is your kitchen still open?" I finally question.

The man behind the bar nods. "Yup."

With this, their huddle separates a bit, two of the men relaxing into their seats at the bar while the guy in the cowboy hat staggers off into another room. There's something awkward about his walk, and I can't help letting my gaze follow his strange, jaunty movements.

The bartender notices. "He'll be fine," the man states. "He's been thinking he's a real life cowboy for the last hour."

A wave of concern washes over me, only amplified by the sight of an old six-shooter gun hanging on a mantle behind the bar. I'm guessing it's a prop, but according to Chekhov, this is a bad sign.

"Is he vaccinated?" I question, motioning toward the cowboy.

The bartender nods reassuringly, a gesture that would've been convincing if not for the fact that he did it so quickly.

"Oh yeah, not to worry," the bartender confirms. "We're all vaccinated, right boys?"

The guys sitting at the bar nod.

One of them, the man in the trucker hat, hoists his drink toward us. "Where you folks from?"

"LA," Nora replies. "Where are *you* from?"

"About a hundred yards that way. Up on the hill," he reveals, hitching a thumb over his shoulder and smiling. There's something unexpectedly charming about this guy, a playful warmth in his demeanor that I didn't see coming.

"Shouldn't y'all be hunkered down in Palm Springs for the evening?" the man asks.

Nora's eyes widen. "Excuse me?" she snarls. "What makes you think that?"

The guy in the trucker's hat is startled by her

reaction, immediately struggling to backtrack. "I mean... I don't know... I just kinda figured-"

"I'm just messing with you," Nora blurts, cracking a mischievous grin.

"We're gay as fuck," Jason chimes in, a moment of levity from my otherwise somber friend.

The guy in the trucker hat smiles and chuckles to himself. "Alright, you got me."

"Palm Springs is tough to get into if you're not a resident," Jason continues. "Costs around forty-five grand for the night."

"I saw some artillery trucks with them rainbow flags," the man's friend finally chimes in, nodding along. "Got the place locked up tight. I'm Brandon, by the way."

He gives a friendly nod.

"Ricky," the man in the trucker hat offers.

We make our introductions, smiling and shaking hands.

"What brings you guys out tonight?" I question. "It's a ghost town."

"Business is so damn slow they're *paying us* to drink here," Ricky replies. He takes a long sip from his beer.

"They work here," the bartender explains. "I own the joint."

As he says this he gazes into the other room, his eyes falling upon the wobbling cowboy who's now making his way from table to table with that strange, jangly walk. Suddenly, the cowboy stops and straightens up, frozen in place as he stares at the wall.

It's a nice reminder that we shouldn't be wasting any more time.

"Alright let's make our orders," I announce to my friends, grabbing a few laminated menus from a stack on the bar and passing them out.

"Are we doing drinks first and then food?" I question.

"No drinks," Nora interjects, her eyes transfixed on the cowboy in the other room. "Let's get some food and hit the road."

***

"I think it's just over this ridge," Hazel announces, glancing down at her phone and then comparing her map to the winding dirt road before us. "My service is a little spotty out here."

We're creeping along now, the car quaking and trembling as we rumble our way down a dusty path. Any semblance of civilization is long gone, replaced instead by hills and valleys that are completely covered by namesake Joshua trees in all their glory.

Of course, we're not *completely* alone. Off to the left there's a single other cabin resting at the top of the far hill. It's several miles away, but I catch someone standing on the front porch, watching us pass.

"Creepy old guy alert," I offer, pointing.

Nora leans over and gazes out my window. "Ooo, is he holding a chainsaw? Is that a hockey mask?"

"Stop," Jason blurts.

"He is!" Nora cries out. "He's got the head of Cara Delevingne on a stick!"

She abruptly quiets down.

"Wait. Actually, that guy is super creepy," Nora finally admits.

We don't stop to confirm that he is, in fact, super creepy, continuing around the bend to find our cabin nestled against a rocky hillside. The place is nice, and a little larger than it looked in the pictures. There's even a hot tub in back, which I suppose we could use if we keep the lights off and stay relatively quiet.

Jason parks and we immediately get to work, climbing out of the car and pulling an assortment of dark sheets from the trunk. Thankfully, what we lack in groceries, we make up for in zombie avoidance tactics.

Obviously, boarding up the place would be the most effective precaution, but you can't go putting nails in the window frames of your Airbnb and expect to maintain a five star rating. The next best thing is an assortment of thick black sheets, which will keep our already minimal light sources muted to the outside world.

We drop off our bags in each of the rooms. Nora and Hazel take the back, while Jason settles in the front bedroom and I hoist my duffle into a cozy little loft above the living area. Next, I pop open a small plastic container of thumb tacks and the gang gets to work hanging sheets over the windows and doors.

"The sooner we finish this, the sooner we can chill," I announce, the very thought of relaxing on a night like this feeling utterly comical the second it leaves my lips.

Up until this point I really wasn't sure if the trip was a good idea. It's hard to predict what tonight will bring, landing somewhere between a handful of news stories that barely catch the world's collective attention, to a complete meltdown of society as we know it.

There are so many ways to play your cards.

Should I have stayed in Los Angeles, praying my liberal neighbors actually took some precautions to keep me alive? Should I have saved up all year for a Palm Springs ticket, lounging by the pool while a DJ spins top forty dance tracks?

Or does it even matter? Is the third anniversary of Saturation Day going to be remembered as the one everyone finally got their shit together?

Soon enough, our group has settled in, the furniture repositioned to block our windows and ready to barricade the front and back doors at a moment's notice. Without any couches or chairs left, we've gathered on the living room floor, sitting in a circle like this is our very first night in a brand new home. As the sun edges closer and closer to the distant horizon line, Jason, Nora and I break out the board games while Hazel messes with something in her bedroom.

"Baby, let's go!" Nora calls out. "We're ready to play!"

"Keep it down," Jason reminds her in a hushed tone. "You're yelling."

"It's not eight yet!" Nora protests.

"We still don't want anyone to know we're here," I chime in.

Nora rolls her eyes.

Suddenly, a cacophonous buzz erupts from the other room, causing the three of us to jump in alarm. I scramble to my feet and back away from the hallway, my heart slamming in my chest as I struggle to identify the source.

It sounds like a whirring saw blade.

"Hazel?" I call out.

From down the hallway, a shadow drifts into my field of vision. It takes a moment for this object to register, but the second it does I melt into a state of utter relief and gratitude. A small black drone is floating in the air before me at eye level, humming loudly as it holds position with startling accuracy.

Hazel strolls out behind her arial robot, glancing between the machine and a visual display on her phone.

"Where's the marching band?" Jason sighs, throwing his hands up as he shakes his head with frustration.

"What?" Hazel calls out over the buzz of her drone.

"Exactly!" Jason shouts.

"Don't worry, I won't use it after eight," Hazel explains. "Too dark then. I just wanted to get some footage of the desert. I'll take it up high. Nobody's gonna know it's there."

"Is it really the best time for this?" I ask.

"Perfect timing, actually," Hazel retorts. "Think of it as our very own, state of the art security system. We'll get a lay of the land, see what's out there."

It's not the worst idea I've ever heard, especially when framed like that. While the drone can't see anything after dark, it might come in handy before things fully lock down.

Besides, I can't help feeling just a *little* bit curious about the man on the other hillside.

"I'm cool with it," I finally proclaim.

"I'm not," Jason reaffirms.

Nora shrugs. "Looks like it's three against one."

Jason sits for a moment, just shaking his head from side to side and then finally standing up from his cross legged position on the floor. Without a word, he heads off into the back room and shuts the door behind him.

Nora grimaces before breaking out in a fit of giggles, struggling to stay quiet as she covers her mouth and rolls onto the floor.

"Okay, okay," I stammer, hoping to calm her down. "It's a stressful day. He's right, you know. We shouldn't be fucking around."

Hazel perks up. "We're not fucking around," she reminds me. "We're gathering information."

It's not long before we open the front door and watch as Hazel's humming drone drifts into the warm desert air. Nora waves goodbye as we close the door behind it, turning our attention to the phone held tight within Hazel's grip.

From here we get a live, point-of-view feed from the hovering robot, seeing through its camera eyes as Hazel pilots the machine. I now notice a simple hardware device has been wrapped around my friend's phone, allowing her better controls while piloting the drone.

"Here we go," Hazel announces, causing the machine to blast upward with incredible speed.

Her drone rockets toward the sky, the cabin entering its field of vision and gradually becoming smaller and smaller as the drone gazes down from this position above. The camera turns slowly, sweeping upward before panning across the wide open desert.

STRAIGHT

Shadows are long now, causing the rare trees and shrubs of this desolate landscape to cast thin silhouettes for miles across the yellow dirt. Regardless of our informational mission, I can see why Hazel wanted to capture a bit of this natural wonder on video.

The drone begins to make its way across this vast open landscape, taking in spectacular views as it finds a cruising altitude. Our eyes are transfixed on the screen, feeling as though we're hovering up there ourselves.

"That's the road we came in on," Hazel observes, passing over the winding dirt lane that curves along a steep, rocky hillside. She follows it for a good while, watching intently until it flattens out several miles to the East.

I have to admit, getting a bird's eye view like this is rather calming. Our whole plan was based around avoiding civilization, but it's hard to fully grasp just how desolate this place really is until you see it for yourself.

I already feel much, much safer.

Eventually, Hazel swings the drone back around and takes a straight shot toward the house on the opposing ridge.

"He's not gonna hear the drone coming?" I question.

"I'll keep it high," Hazel assures me. "Even if he *does* hear, he's not gonna know where it came from."

It's not long before the drone is hovering directly above this mysterious man's rickety old cabin, a cosmic eye gazing down from the heavens in search of something demonic and finding, well, nothing.

I hold my breath as the camera zooms in, expecting us to be treated to some horrific, bizarre scene, but that doesn't happen. Sure, the place is a mess, large objects strewn about the property like an automotive junkyard, but the closer our field of vision draws, the more the true nature of these structures is revealed. They're sculptures, salvaged materials that were painted, welded and repurposed into strange works of funky desert art.

"Aww," Nora gushes. "He's an *artist.*"

Our watchful lens finally discovers the man himself. He's sitting in front of an old car bumper and delicately covering it with thick, yellow paint. This piece is part of a larger edifice, car parts fused to resemble a humanoid figure.

"That dude's a liberal," Nora continues. "He's *painting.* You know he got the vaccine."

"Some old folks can't get it," I remind her.

"He's not *that* old," Hazel observes. "The cut off is seventy-five. This guy's in his fifties. Not even close."

We observe him paint a while longer, falling into a strangely peaceful silence. There's a certain calm to this moment of aerial voyeurism, and I don't push back against it. None of us do.

Finally, Hazel lifts the drone and starts the process of bringing her little robot home.

We really *are* in the middle of nowhere, and while this is something I'd known in the depths of my logical brain, all of the chaos and tension of this day hadn't let me fully accept it. Now, seeing with my own eyes just how far this desert stretches on and on around us, I've settled into a new mood.

Everything's gonna be fine. We're on vacation.

3

The door of Jason's room is open just a crack when I approach, but I take my time entering. It feels as though I'm creeping into a lion's den, careful not to disturb the beast.

My friend is sitting upright on the bed, his legs crossed over one another and his back pressed against the wall. There's a book in his hands, and while I'm certain he's noticed my arrival, Jason doesn't look up from the page.

I wait for a solid minute, wondering if Jason will finish the paragraph and turn his attention toward me. He doesn't.

"Nice shorts" Jason finally offers, his eyes still glued to the paperback.

I glance down, as if to confirm that I am, in fact, wearing nice shorts.

"Yeah," I reply. "We're getting in the hot tub for sunset. You wanna come?"

Jason turns the page. "I'd ask if you're joking, but I

see you've already got your suit on and there's a towel over your shoulder."

I nod, receiving the answer I fully expected to get. Still, that's not the only reason I came to talk.

Finally, Jason puts his book down. "On the first Desaturation Day I was out with Mark. We were walking down the street, drunk off our asses, and we were headed to that frozen yogurt place on the corner of Santa Monica and Palm. I just wanted to go home, but Mark always wanted dessert when he was wasted."

Jason stops for a moment, just staring at the wall in front of him.

Watching this kind of emotion bubble up is even more devastating within the man's large frame. He's holding it together, but barely.

"Anyway, we get there and everyone's gathered around the front window looking in. People are screaming for help, or gasping or, no joke, fainting," Jason explains, suddenly cracking a smile as his eyes well with tears. "Someone actually *fainted*, I didn't think that could happen in real life. I figured it was kinda like hitting someone in the head to knock them out; they do it in every other movie but I doubt it would work if you tried it."

"What were they looking at?" I ask.

Jason clears his throat, centering himself again as he continues staring at the wall. It's as though the whole scene is playing out on some old news reel in his mind, projected into reality for only Jason to see.

"We pushed through the crowd. I think we figured it was someone losing their shit after one too many tequila shots. We were laughing, trying to get a better view, you know?" Jason explains. "Then I got up to the window and saw the blood. It was everywhere. The girl behind the counter had someone sliced open, and the body was just lying there in front of her, next to the toppings. She was shoveling everything from his chest cavity into one of those little bins. Made a huge mess. I guess she thought someone might want it on their froyo."

Jason blinks a few times, then turns his gaze toward me.

"I recognized the guy. He was our dog walker," he continues. "Where were you on the first Desaturation Day?"

"My brother was visiting town," I offer flatly, the pool of blood on my living room floor suddenly flashing into the forefront of my mind. "He's straight."

I consider correcting this phrase to the past tense, but I can't bring myself to do it.

Jason knew this short story of mine, but I guess he'd forgotten. He's been so focused on how tragic these events were in his own life, that he's completely neglected we all went through the same thing. This wasn't a tragedy for any *one person,* it was a tragedy for the entire community.

A single tear rolls down my friend's face and he wipes it away.

"I'm sorry," he continues. "I'm not trying to be a buzz kill, but this is a serious time."

"Sometimes the best way to deal with something serious is to get a little silly," I remind him. "You can't just exercise these demons by moping around. Well, maybe you can, but *I* can't. Nora *certainly* can't."

"I know, I know," Jason continues. "You've gotta

understand, though. If this was a horror movie, everyone would be so fucking frustrated by the three of you. I'm the only one who's actually prepared."

"You forgot the groceries," I counter.

"I forgot the market and gas station *closed early,*" Jason retorts, correcting me. "I still brought supplies."

I stare at him blankly, struggling to understand what he's getting at and then finally letting it slide. It seems like we've reached a nice middle ground here, a level of mutual respect rather than any specific compromise.

That's worth something.

"The audience might be frustrated," I finally offer, "but I refuse to live like I'm a character in a horror movie. Not anymore."

Jason nods respectfully, then turns his attention back to the book in his hands. I notice now that it's some pulpy, zombie apocalypse paperback. "Don't stay out too long after sundown," Jason offers.

I turn and leave, making my way down the hall and pushing out through the back door of the cabin.

The second I emerge from the darkness of this covered-window structure, I'm greeted by one of the most breathtaking sunsets I've ever witnessed. The sky has blossomed into a stunning canvas of purples and oranges, radiating from the sun that just barely peeks over a distant hillside.

"Whoa," I blurt, the word falling unexpectedly from my mouth in a flat exhale.

The light pollution is so low out here that glorious cascades of stars are already sparkling to life, coming into view within the depths of the darkest indigos.

STRAIGHT

Back on Earth, a hot tub sits calm and quiet some twenty yards out from the house, its warm water lapping quietly as Nora and Hazel relax within. They're wrapped in each other's arms, staring up at the evening sky as I approach. Cans of beer sit precariously on the ledge next to them.

When my friends notice me they smile, but they don't call out a greeting. We're staying quiet, not just from an abundance of caution, but in some kind of cosmic respect for the silence of this wide open desert around us. Even the jacuzzi jets are turned off.

I reach the tub and strip away my shirt, placing this article and my dry towel to the side. I gingerly climb in, gasping as the simmering water touches my skin and then slipping down below the surface. It's the perfect temperature, a heat that teases the edge of *too much* at first blush and then gradually evens out the longer you soak.

"How's he doing?" Hazel questions, her voice hushed.

"He'll be fine," I reply. "I get it. He's worried. I'm worried, too."

"We all are," Hazel confirms. "We just express it in different ways."

The three of us lean back in our seats and watch as the sky gradually changes color above, shifting into darker and darker shades. Soon enough, the whole thing is fully bathed in brilliant, sparkling stars.

"Sokos 12 reached The Blank Space," Hazel informs me, her eyes still transfixed on the glorious display above.

"Oh yeah?" I question. "That's the probe, right?"

"Yep," Hazel continues. "Apparently, the size and shape of The Blank Space has changed."

I sit up a bit, gravely concerned despite the fact that Hazel and Nora don't seem to care in the slightest.

"What does that mean?" I ask.

Hazel smiles. "I don't know."

I let out a deep breath, sliding back into my cozy, submerged nook. I realize now that, despite Hazel's incredible technical intelligence, the most impressive thing about her is her emotional fortitude. She's smart enough to know there are some things we just don't understand, at least not yet.

"As a scientist, have the last few years been frustrating?" I ask.

Hazel scoffs. "They've been frustrating *as a human being.*"

"True," I admit. "It seems like we had all these laws, right? Physics, biology, astronomy. We've been cruising along for thousands of years and building on this knowledge without realizing it's a house of cards. One day, a tear in the sky comes along and tells us only half of those cards ever really existed."

Hazel considers my words for a moment. "Honestly, it's kind of exciting," she replies. "I feel weird saying that."

"Yeah," I confirm, understanding completely.

So much death and destruction has unfolded around us over the last few years, it's hard to see it through any other lens than one of overwhelming, devastating tragedy. The queer community went from small and marginalized to practically extinct, but at the same time people started respecting us tenfold.

I suppose that's bound to happen when every queer person in power is simultaneously outed across the globe on the same day.

Regardless, I understand what Hazel's getting at. These are unquestionably tragic circumstances, but you can't stay inside with sheets hanging over the windows forever. At a certain point, you've gotta come out here and start gazing at the stars again.

There's a whole new set of rules now, a whole new reality waiting to be navigated, and while this fresh world is certainly frightening, I'm glad to be working through it with friends by my side.

"I think it's over," Nora finally announces. She's been unusually quiet, but after giving it a lot of thought my friend has decided to let her perspective be known. "I think the first year was horrible, the second year we started to figure things out, and this year we're barely gonna notice."

"People are clearly still affected" I counter. "We've seen plenty of weirdos today."

"But they're not killing anyone," Nora continues. "If straight people wanna take off their clothes and bumble around like zombie cowboys one night a year then I say let 'em. Honestly, they could use the fun."

"She's right, actually," Hazel chimes in. "Even after receiving the vaccine, many patients still display unusual behavior when nearing the field of influence. It doesn't necessarily mean they'll enter an aggressive state later on."

"At least, that's what happened last year," I counter.

Hazel nods.

"And The Blank Space has a new shape," I continue.

Hazel nods again. "But, there's no reason to think that will make any difference."

"We're so fucked," I reply, chuckling to myself as I gaze up at the sky above.

It's dark now. We should probably head inside, but there's still a few minutes left to enjoy this moment.

"Why can't I see some big weird hole when I look up into the sky?' I question, my eyes dancing from one sparkling pinpoint to the next. "Shouldn't a patch of stars be missing or something?"

"The Blank Space is empty," Nora chimes in, clearly parroting one of Hazel's frequently answered questions. "It's not matter and it's not energy. You're not seeing it because it doesn't exist, but your mind is filling in the blanks."

I furrow my brow. "What does that even *mean?*"

"Uh... pass," Nora blurts.

"There's nothing for light to reflect off of, so technically we shouldn't be able to see it," Hazel jumps in to explain. "The thing is, humans have trouble perceiving true *nothingness*. Darkness, sure, but nothing is so much more than that, or less depending on the way you look at it. You know how the whole universe was once a tiny little speck, and then suddenly The Big Bang erupted out of that singularity? What do you think was surrounding the tiny little speck?"

"Outer space?" I reply. "A barren universe?"

Hazel shakes her head. "The *universe* is the speck, remember. Surrounding it is, well, nothingness."

STRAIGHT

"Blank space," I offer.

"Yes, a void," Hazel continues. "We can't imagine what that *really* means, so we picture darkness. We fill it in with something that makes sense. When you look up at the stars on Saturation Day, that's exactly what's happening. Your brain is filling it in so you can perceive the unperceivable."

"So, part of this view isn't real?" I curiously ask, speaking more to myself than anyone else.

Nora sits up. "Maybe *none* of it is real," she interjects, the tone in her voice immediately causing me to roll my eyes. I know exactly what's about to happen here, a conversation I've been subjected to many times in the past, and will likely have to deal with well into the future.

Nora's a little buzzed, and that's when the conspiracy theories start coming out.

"How can you date her?" I chide Hazel with a knowing smirk. By now, Hazel and Nora are just two dark silhouettes, their features barely visible under the natural light from above.

Nora laughs. "It's because deep down she knows it's *possible.*"

"This is not all fake," Hazel retorts.

"What if all the straight people got together and decided to just *wipe us out,*" Nora continues, clearly excited to dole out the same tired nonsense we've already heard a thousand times. "They're just pretending to be overwhelmed so they can *straighten out the world* once and for all."

"So like... even your mom and dad are faking the homicidal maniac thing?" I continue. "They're in on this, too?"

"Alright, fine," Nora blurts, a little too loud. "Fuck!"

Hazel and me both erupt with frustrated shushes, struggling to quiet our friend. Regardless, Nora keeps rolling along, albeit at a slightly lowered volume.

"What about this one?" she offers. "You know how everyone used to talk about the *gay gene?* How nature is straight and then with every few people God just sprinkled on a little queerness?"

"That's one way of putting it," I chuckle, "but sure."

"What if they've been looking at it all wrong?" she offers. "What if thousands of years ago we were *all* queer, and some alien virus caused an infection of *straightness*. What if The Blank Space is a rip that leads to another world and those aliens are coming back to reactivate their latent strain of straight zombie rage!"

Hazel and I sit silently for a moment.

"Honestly, I'd buy it," I admit.

The three of us start laughing, then abruptly quiet ourselves down.

"We should probably head inside," I finally suggest. "It's about that time."

I start climbing out of the hot tub but immediately freeze, my vision locked onto something ten or so yards behind Hazel and Nora. My breath catches in my throat as my logical brain struggles to calm me down, explaining away this shadowy form as a large, slender cactus that I just hadn't noticed yet.

"I think I see something," I whimper, my voice

even quieter than our already established hush.

"What?" Nora questions, unable to hear me now that I've descended into a mumble.

My eyes are glued to the figure in the darkness, struggling to make sense of what I'm seeing. The object is standing perfectly still, but every so often I sense a faint twitch of movement.

"Is that a cactus or a person?" I question.

Slowly, Hazel and Nora turn around to follow my gaze. Now all three of us are staring into the open desert, completely still as we struggle to remember if this unnerving object was actually there the whole time.

Nobody says a word, the whole gang slowly waiting for our eyes to adjust as icy terror seeps its way into our warm bodies. My heart is slamming in my chest as I'm filled with disappointed ache, wishing I'd taken all this just a little more seriously.

Nothing's gonna happen tonight, I remind myself. *It's getting better. Everyone took the vaccine and it's working.*

Finally, Nora breaks the tension, turning back toward me. "Now you sound just like Jason. There's nobody out here."

She reaches over and grabs her beer can, which is now mostly empty and crinkles slightly under the pressure of her fingers. She takes a moment to aim, then makes a powerful overhand throw at the object.

It's too dark to see much of anything, but the glint of the moon catches Nora's aluminum can as it sails through the air. It strikes the mysterious figure with a direct hit.

Nothing happens.

The can clatters to the ground, revealing this frightening stranger to likely be nothing more than a cactus that wasn't worth noticing until things got scary.

I let out a sigh of relief, the tension within my body immediately dissipating.

"You need to go pick that up," I inform Nora, then soften a bit. "In the morning."

Suddenly, the figure in the darkness rushes toward us. It happens so fast that I barely have time to cry out, the reptilian part of my brain immediately taking hold and causing me to erupt from the water. I tumble backward, trying my best to stay upright but flipping over the tub's slippery plastic edge in a plume of sloshing liquid.

Pain surges through my shoulder as I slam against the hard dirt. I can hear the ladies screaming as more water erupts over the edge, hissing while it spreads across the dry dirt.

I scramble to my feet as Nora and Hazel join me, rushing back toward the cabin. Behind us, the figure is still approaching, moving through the darkness like a shark. The form is large and, now that it's moving, it glistens under the moonlight as though it's covered in something reflective.

"Jason!" I scream. "Open the door!"

Our bare feet pound the dirt, soft soles pierced by sharp rocks and prickly weeds that we promptly ignore. Right now, I have a singular focus: making sure everyone gets inside safely.

We're a few steps from the cabin door when another silhouette emerges from the darkness, blocking our path.

Nora, who's in the lead, pulls back with a startled

yelp, punching this large shape in the jaw and then swiftly altering course along the wall of the cabin.

A lantern erupts to life, the pale glow bursting into existence and illuminating the frightening face of Ricky, the man from the saloon. His expression is twisted into a bizarre grin, the smile stretched so wide that I probably wouldn't recognize him if not for the familiar trucker's hat he'd been sporting earlier.

The man is shirtless, and his body is absolutely covered in dark red blood. He holds a baseball bat by his side, the weapon also smeared in this crimson substance.

"Front door!" I cry out, but Hazel and Nora are way ahead of me, hustling around the side of the cabin.

The figures are marching along behind us as we sprint through the darkness. Ricky begins to scream, repeating the same phrase over and over again in a wild shriek.

"Can I help you? Can I help you? Can I help you?" the man cries out, his voice echoing through the desert.

We've pulled ahead now, his voice growing fainter as we round the second corner and rush toward the cabin's front door. Hazel gets there first, throwing it open and barreling inside as Nora and I follow. The door slams hard behind us, and I lock the deadbolt as Jason emerges from the bedroom.

Jason's eyes are wild as he struggles to understand what's happening.

"Someone's out there," Nora yells.

"Someone?" Jason continues. "Overwhelmed?"

"Yes!" Nora cries. "Two of them!"

"They might not be overwhelmed," I blurt. "We

don't know if they're actually trying to hurt us. Maybe they're just confused."

"What the fuck are you talking about?" Nora screams. "They were covered in *blood*. One of them was carrying a bat!"

The second Jason hears this he storms into the other room.

Meanwhile, Hazel is pulling on her clothes. She tosses a bag to Nora. "Get dressed," she offers, always thinking logically. "The desert gets cold at night. Put on your running shoes."

I rush over to the windows and pull back a dark sheet, peering outside. The figures have vanished.

Now that I've got a moment to think, I follow the ladies lead, finding my duffle bag and quickly pulling on my clothes. I'd expected these running shoes to come in handy when I got up early and went for a jog, but now they might save my life.

Once they're finished getting ready, Nora and Hazel start pushing the furniture into position before both doors, sealing us in. They're just about finished blocking off the front entrance with a couch when Jason returns. He's brandishing a hunting rifle.

"Whoa!" I blurt, shocked by the sight of the weapon.

"I told you I came prepared," he announces.

Jason pushes past the ladies and begins hauling the couch out of his way, attempting to head outside.

"Wait, wait," I cry. "What are you going to do, shoot them?"

"We're under attack," he snarls.

STRAIGHT

"We're not!" I counter, grabbing Jason's shoulder and stopping him in his tracks. "Even if we are, it's not their fault. They didn't choose this!"

"They didn't get the vaccine," Jason continues. *"That's a choice."*

Now it's time for Hazel to interject. "Not necessarily, there's a lot of factors at play here. The Blank Space changed shape, and different people are affected in different ways. Last year, several-"

"Hey!" Nora snaps abruptly, grabbing everyone's attention. She's gazing out the window into our moonlit front yard. "They're back."

The rest of us hurry over and push the sheet away, crowding around the window. Ricky and his companion—who I now recognize as Brandon, the other guy from the bar—are standing motionless. Brandon is holding their battery powered lantern now, while Ricky maintains his grip on the crimson-smeared bat.

Both of them are shirtless and absolutely covered in blood, the same bizarre grins still plastered across their faces.

"Hut, hut, hike! Hut, hut, hike!" Ricky begins screaming at the top of his lungs, his eyes wide.

Nora's frown has taken over her entire face. "I'll never understand straight people," is all that she says.

A loud crash suddenly rings through the cabin as Jason tears the sofa away from the front door. The couch slams against the ground as our friend barrels outside and raises his rifle at the two intruders.

Immediately, the expressions on Brandon and Ricky's faces change. They're terrified.

"Wait, wait, wait!" Ricky cries out, his words tumbling over themselves as they all struggle to exit his mouth at the same time. "We were just fucking around! Don't shoot!"

My friends and I freeze in the doorway, utterly dumbfounded.

Jason doesn't lower his gun. "Why the fuck are you covered in blood?" he demands to know.

"It's fake," Brandon immediately chimes in. "My cousin does effects work in Hollywood. I think it's corn syrup."

Both groups stand awkwardly for a moment, not sure what to make of this bizarre situation. I'm thankful these two intruders aren't belligerent, rage-filled zombies, but in some ways this new revelation is even more disappointing.

"Tell me why I shouldn't just shoot you in the fucking head," Jason suddenly blurts.

I glance over to see his hands are trembling as he grips the rifle tightly, his finger dancing dangerously close to the trigger. This whole experience has been an emotional pressure cooker for Jason, and I realize now with terrifying clarity that it's seconds away from a mighty bang.

I lower my voice a bit, taking on a soft, calming tone. "Hey, they're not overwhelmed," I offer. "They're just idiots."

"They knew what they were doing," he states firmly. "That's even worse."

This simple phrase sends a shockwave through my body. I hadn't looked at it like that, but Jason is absolutely right. If these two *were* overwhelmed by The Blank Space, at least they'd have an excuse for their actions.

Still, it's not worth murdering them over.

"Put the gun down," I finally continue.

Jason takes a deep breath and then, at long last, he lowers the weapon.

A visible wave of relief washes over Ricky and Brandon, their muscles relaxing as the immediate danger subsides.

"That was a really dumb idea," I call over to them. "Why the hell would you do that?"

"We're just having fun," Ricky retorts, immediately discovering some irreverent confidence now that he's no longer looking down the barrel of a gun. "It's not a big deal."

"It's a huge deal," I snap. "Do you know how many people died on Saturation Day?"

"Yeah, *two years ago,*" Ricky counters. "Then last year it was a quarter of that, and this year everyone's gonna be fine. Even us desert folk got the vaccine, see? It's over."

Nora pushes her way to the front of the group. "You're a dick," she calls out, then steps back into the cabin before lowering her voice to a hushed whisper. "I told you all the straights were faking it."

Back in the yard, it appears Brandon is still not fully on board with this little adventure, his body language suggesting he was dragged along for the ride. He shifts awkwardly from side to side as his friend does the talking, unable to make eye contact out of sheer embarrassment.

"You leftist globalist cucks take everything way too seriously," Ricky continues. "Cancel culture has ruined you."

"How do you know we're leftists?" Jason questions, the gun in his hand making a reasonable case for the contrary.

Ricky smirks, the mischievous confidence within him growing even more. He loudly spits, making a big show of it as though laying claim to the yellow dirt before him. It's clear the man has now realized Jason isn't going to shoot, his fear gradually transforming into frustrated aggression.

"Fine, you fuckin' *queers,*" he continues, pushing the envelope even more.

I grimace as he says this.

Nora steps forward again. "You can't say that," she informs him. *"We* can say it. You can't."

Ricky raises an eyebrow. "What word should I use then? I can think of a few."

A figure emerges from the darkness behind Ricky, marching up and shoving a pitchfork through the back of his neck.

It happens so fast, and with such nonchalance, that it takes my brain a full second to register what just happened. The whole world seems to halt.

Suddenly, everyone is screaming as Ricky staggers forward with three massive metal forks protruding from the flesh around his Adam's apple. Behind him stands our neighbor from the opposing hillside, the man's shirt now covered in splatters of blood. He's wearing a leather belt full of brushes and some metalworking tools, and his face is covered with brilliant white paint to create an even more horrific visage.

Ricky falls forward, slamming into the dirt as the

white-faced man turns his attention toward us.

"Inside!" I cry out, pushing back into the cabin.

The artist doesn't waste any time, emitting a blood-curdling shriek and charging toward Jason.

There's a deafening bang as my friend raises his weapon and takes his shot. A bullet slams into the artist's shoulder, but it barely slows him down. The next thing I know, this paint and blood splattered assailant is tackling Jason, knocking him back into the cabin and landing on top of him with a hearty thud.

Jason's rifle goes flying, sliding across the wooden floor and down the nearby hallway.

Still howling, the crazed straight man sits up and reaches for his tool belt, finding a cordless hand saw and pulling it forth with a single spastic jerk. The tool whirrs to life with a loud, cacophonous buzz as he raises it into the air, ready to bring the humming blade down onto Jason's face until, suddenly, he's cracked on the side of the head with a bat.

The artist is knocked prone as Brandon stands triumphant over him, but his victory doesn't last long. A blow to the head would've likely killed any typical human outright, but whatever hate-filled adrenaline now pumps through the artist's veins has made him damn near unstoppable.

I watch in horror, backing away as the zombie climbs to his feet.

The man's skull is caved in slightly, but he doesn't seem to notice. Anger is the only thing his mind has room for at the moment.

"Come on," Hazel shouts, grabbing me and pulling

me toward the nearby ladder. She and Nora are already halfway up it, climbing into the cabin's loft.

I follow their lead, helping up Jason as all four of us frantically scramble to safety.

Brandon, as far as I know, is straight, and from what I understand about the overwhelmed, they'll basically ignore him in their attempts to get at us. That theory, however, doesn't account for what happens when you smash one across the skull with a baseball bat.

Now, the artist's focus is torn between following us up the ladder and retaliating against that home run swing.

The artist shrieks and lunges at Brandon once again, taking a second crack from the baseball bat and shrugging it off completely. He keeps coming, leaping onto Brandon and prompting me to halt my ascent.

I'm the last one up before my friends and I have escaped to relative safety, but I just can't leave this guy behind.

Despite the cries of Nora, Hazel and Jason, I turn around and rush back toward the artist. Without a weapon in hand, I do the first thing I can think of and kick him hard in the side. It's not much, but it's somehow enough for Brandon to harness this momentum and push the zombie off of him.

The artist shrieks, scrambling to his feet and barreling after us as Brandon and I take off running toward the ladder. I leap upward from the third rung as my friends reach out and grab me. Brandon follows close behind, kicking at the artist as this squealing maniac tries to pull him down.

Fortunately—and thanks to a few more helping

hands—Brandon is guided up over the edge. The artist attempts to climb the ladder after him, but we swiftly push it back and cause the whole thing to come toppling over. The zombie lands with a thud in the middle of the living room, his screams echoing through the desert for a good while until eventually dying down.

Now, all five of us are crammed into this tiny loft, gazing down at our pursuer as we struggle to collect ourselves.

"Oh my god," Jason blurts. "The gun. He's gonna just find it and shoot us."

"That depends," Hazel interjects. "Does he shoot guns in his normal life? Is that a hobby of his? The overwhelmed are a mix of rage and habit, and when those particular brain areas are firing this ferociously, the logical ones fall away."

"So he's not smart enough to use the gun?" I question.

"While overwhelmed? Maybe, maybe not," she replies. "He hasn't gone for it yet, though."

"How the hell do you know so much about this stuff?" Brandon interjects.

Hazel turns toward him with quiet ferocity.

"I *have* to know about this stuff," she replies.

The real meaning of this comment doesn't even register with Brandon, but everyone else in the group understands completely.

4

Down on the ground floor, the artist begins to shuffle around. He stares at us as we gaze down from above, smiling wide while blood continues to wick out across his chest and shoulder. It's spilling forth from his fresh bullet wound. The dent in the side of his head is even more apparent now, and I'm sickened by the thought of what permanent damage might've been done.

Despite the fact that we were fighting for our lives, I'm still concerned for this confused, rage-filled man. I can't help but think of my brother as our gaze meets, my eyes overflowing with tragic recognition and his bloodshot with frightening, vein-popping anger.

His expression is truly one to behold, a wide smile conveying some kind of sick joy in this destruction. I know he's not acting under his own control, but it's difficult not to feel the hint of some deeper fury in a face like that.

Eventually, the artist springs into action, finding a coffee table and placing it at the center of the room. He then makes his way into the kitchen and starts pulling open drawers with a series of loud clatters.

"What the hell is he doing?" Nora questions aloud.

Nobody has an answer, but the commotion downstairs continues as the artist goes about his business. He's opening cupboards and tearing down the dishes, smashing plates across the floor before gathering up shards and dumping them onto the coffee table.

The artist stares at his handiwork a moment, jerking his head wildly from side to side before he starts belligerently screaming once again.

Eventually, I turn my attention back to our group, taking in a myriad of exhausted, frightened expressions. Everyone is struggling to collect themselves, sorting through the rapid fire of horrific events that just took place.

Brandon looks particularly shaken up, staring at the wall in wide-eyed shock as he processes the death of his friend.

"Something's wrong," Hazel announces, staring down at her phone. "Either a *huge* percentage of people lied about getting the vaccine this year, or that shift in The Blank Space has produced ineffective results in a large portion of patients."

She's scrolling through a variety of news sites, doing her best to keep up with the barrage of fresh information as it comes cascading in. I'm more than a little impressed, recognizing the fact that I'd never be able to find that kind of focus at a time like this.

"So what do we do?" I blurt, a rather broad question but the only one that comes to mind.

Hazel ignores me, her eyes glued to the screen as

she frantically skims a wall of text.

"Isn't there that app for people who need help on Saturation Day?" I question.

Hazel scoffs, still reading but giving me just enough attention to dismiss the idea.

"It crashed thirty seconds after changeover," she informs me. "Even if it did work, what kind of help would someone send? The gay militia? They've got their hands full."

"Everyone's on their own tonight," Jason muses.

"Well, we've got each other," Nora chimes in, then nods toward Brandon, "and this fucking guy."

Jason claps loudly, an idea suddenly erupting through the conscious realm of his mind. "This guy!" he blurts. *"This guy* is our ticket out of here. He's straight!"

Brandon's wild-eyed gaze finally breaks away from the wall, his line of sight creeping over to Jason in acknowledgement.

"What the hell are you talking about? That freak almost sawed me in half," he blurts.

"The overwhelmed are not drawn to straight targets; there's truckloads of evidence to prove that," Hazel chimes in, finally looking up from her phone, "Problem is, if you get in their way or start a fight, they'll come after you, too."

"Exactly!" Brandon erupts, then veers off a bit. "Wait, no. What about Ricky? He didn't provoke shit!"

My group of friends goes quiet for a moment.

"I think there's some things about Ricky you probably weren't aware of," I suggest.

Brandon scoffs before gradually coming to grips

STRAIGHT

with what I'm saying. The moment he registers the greater context of my comment, however, he immediately shifts into a state of full-on denial.

"What? Are you fucking kidding me?" Brandon cries out in frustration. "Ricky was no-" he hesitates, then tries again. "Ricky was straight as an arrow."

More silence from the skeptical audience.

"Not likely," Hazel finally states, leaving her rebuttal to this pair of simple words.

There's suddenly a loud thud from below, shifting our attention to ground level. We peer over the loft's edge to find the artist has carried Ricky inside and flopped him down at the center of the living room.

Seconds later, the battery-powered saw begins to hum as our zombie artist goes about his business. He severs Ricky's left arm at the elbow, working his way through flesh in bone with joyful enthusiasm. Blood plumes from the body in a fine mist, erupting from the cut and causing half the artist's white painted face to shift into a deep red.

"Ugh," I blurt in revulsion, turning away.

Everyone but Hazel averts their eyes, her curiosity far outweighing any sense of disgust she might have.

"What's he doing?" I question.

"It appears he's building a sculpture," Hazel observes.

I'm struggling to focus as the saw continues to buzz, my mind running through various potential escape routes. There are plenty of distractions, though, not the least of which are my regretful choices leading up to this moment.

Jason, whose abundance of caution had been a sore

spot this entire trip, was right.

"What the fuck are we even doing out here?" I suddenly blurt, scolding myself out loud as frustration overwhelms me. "We're in the middle of nowhere!"

Nora places a comforting hand on my shoulder. "Isaac, if you think *this* is bad, just imagine what it's like in the city right now."

"Not necessarily," Hazel chimes in, her gaze still trained on the macabre scene below us. "From what I was reading, there's a strong correlation between relative order and gay militia presence."

Brandon erupts in a fit of laughter as the man glances from one unamused face to the next. He briefly tries stifling his outburst, then falls apart and admits defeat as a broad, skeptical grin forces its way across his face. "The *gay militia?*"

"You strike me as someone who'd support our troops," Jason counters.

"Yeah, but I mean, *come on,*" Brandon continues. "Taking all the gay marines and putting them into a single Desaturation Day unit?"

"And trans," Hazel interjects, "and non-binary, asexual, lesbian, bi-"

"I get it," Brandon continues. "That's really who you want protecting you at a time like this?"

I stare blankly at this sad, bigoted man, so overwhelmed by the audacity of his words that I barely know how to respond.

Jason's not having it. "If you'd like to test the strength of a gay man, I can do my best to throw you over the edge of this loft," he offers, muscular and imposing.

Brandon hesitates, then nods in acceptance. "Sorry," he replies.

I turn my attention back to Hazel. "So LA is fine?" I question.

"It's all relative," she continues. "We should keep checking the news reports while we can. From the looks of it, Los Angeles is going to vary by neighborhood. West Hollywood and Silverlake are doing alright, but the night's just beginning."

"So we *don't* go back to LA?" I continue, growing panicked and confused. *"Where do we go?"*

"What about Palm Springs?" Nora suggests. "It's super close."

"You've gotta pay to get in," I gently remind my tragically optimistic friend.

"What, they're going to just turn us away to die?" she counters.

"Yes, literally," I flatly reply.

Nora shakes her head. "They'll let us in."

"What makes you think that?" I ask.

"Gotta watch out for your fellow queers," she retorts with so much conviction that I actually find myself believing her. It's a crazy presumption to make, but there's a wild, heartwarming logic to her suggestion.

"How's Palm Springs doing?" I ask Hazel.

"I mean, it's only been five or ten minutes, but from what I saw things we're running smoothly over there," she offers. "You know, I'm not the only reader here, you're welcome to look it up for yourself."

I pull out my phone and start checking the news, only to discover I've lost both internet and satellite service.

From the frustrated groans of my companions, it appears I'm not the only one.

"I figured that was coming," Hazel states knowingly. "For the record—and this isn't just because Nora is the love of my life—I think Palm Springs is a good idea. If we're turned away we can always head to Los Angeles, but it's the safest bet and it's on our way home. Only thing we need now is a car."

"And gas," Jason chimes in.

Fuck. In all the commotion, I'd completely forgotten about this very important detail. Even if we *could* somehow make it past the frightening little art curator down below and get to Jason's car, we're still running on empty. All the gas stations are closed until tomorrow.

I let out a long sigh, shaking my head from side to side as I fall back against the wall in a frustrated slump.

"You need a ride?" Brandon interjects. "I parked my truck just up the road. Four-door. There's room for everyone."

I sit up once more, eyes wide. "Oh shit," I blurt.

Brandon reaches into his pocket and pulls out his keys.

"So you're coming to Palm Springs with us?" Jason asks gruffly.

"It sounds like *you're* the ones coming with *me,*" Brandon counters.

I nod. "Fair enough. Now we've just gotta find a way around this zombie with a power saw."

"Uh, it's a little more complicated than that," Hazel counters, motioning below.

Our gang crawls to the edge and stares down to

discover a lot has changed in the last few minutes. The artist's sculpture is almost complete, a stack of furniture, kitchen utensils and body parts that are slathered in stark white paint. Ricky's severed head is the centerpiece, speared atop this ghoulish structure on the post of a glowing table lamp. His arms and legs jut from the edifice at awkward locations, and what appear to be his intestines are wrapped around it like a string of popcorn placed gently upon a bloody Christmas tree.

This, however, is far from the most alarming sight.

The artist has been joined by three more crazed straights, the overwhelmed family bumbling around our cabin with jaunty, spastic movements and haunting smiles stretched across their faces.

An older woman, who I assume is the artist's wife, shuffles through the kitchen and pours various foods onto the countertop. She's discovered a box of cereal that was here when we arrived, dumping it out and hacking at it with a large knife.

Meanwhile, a young girl staggers back and forth in the living room, wearing a blue dress and sporting shoes that are already stained with dirt and blood. She's talking on her phone, but the words are a strange, garbled mess of syllables and phrases that spill together like teenage word salad.

The most concerning, however, is what I believe to be her younger brother. This boy is staring at the wall, completely motionless other than a faint twitch in his left hand. In the other hand he holds Jason's rifle.

Everyone in the loft pulls back from the ledge.

"Sound carries pretty far in the desert," Hazel

observes.

That's all she needs to say for the rest of us to heed this important point. Our nuclear family is making a hell of a racket down there, the situation evolving from one frightening adversary to three more in a matter of minutes. Who knows how many could be staggering around the house within an hour?

If I didn't already find myself conflicted about violent confrontation with the overwhelmed, I do now. That dent in the side of the artist's head has been drawing my attention ever since it was so abruptly placed there, a reminder of the consequences that will linger well after tonight's events.

I've read and watched enough science fiction and horror to know the world of a fictional zombie apocalypse is a relatively simple place. Those staggering, groaning hordes gradually represent nothing but a sea of dead flesh, and I suppose in the world of *those* stories it's fine. Once you're bitten, you're not coming back

Here, in the real world, they'll regain their faculties in approximately twenty four hours. They won't remember a damn thing, of course, but the consequences of Saturation Day aren't so easily dismissed.

There are plenty of survivors who find the limits of appropriate self-defense significantly loosened tonight, and logically speaking I don't blame them. In fact, I agree.

But logic isn't everything.

It's one thing to say you'd swing the club when a knife-wielding madman is sprinting toward you, some strange unknowable part of your innate queerness driving him into a belligerent rage, but actually doing it is something else entirely.

I've made that call before, and it's something I'd rather not do again. The idea of living with twice this guilt is too much to bear.

Visions of the family's rage-fueled children flood my mind, my soul aching for them as they stagger around our living room.

Did the vaccines fail, or did they opt out entirely? Did their parents fill their heads with conspiracy theories, or was that syringe really chock full of nanobots, allowing the gay mafia to track their every move?

"All that rage makes the overwhelmed pretty damn strong, but I think we can take them," Jason offers in a hushed tone. "There's five of us and only four of them, and they've got two kids. If I can wrestle the gun away from the little one, we'd be in good shape."

"No," I state firmly, the single, abrupt word causing my companions to turn. "We need a plan, but we're not gonna kill anyone."

"Are you fucking insane?" Jason hisses. "First, you all ignore my warnings about staying inside, and now this?"

"They're human beings," I remind him.

"It's really sweet you think of the overwhelmed like that, and it may be true three hundred and sixty-four days a year, but tonight they don't give a damn about you, Isaac," my friend continues.

"I'm not gonna let you hurt any of these people," I retort, holding fast.

"If push comes to shove, I don't know if you can stop us," Jason replies confidently.

"Who's us?" I counter.

Jason looks around at the group. "Should we vote on it?"

"Vote on *what* exactly?" I reply.

Brandon butts in loudly. "On killing these zombie fucks!"

The wind in Jason's sails abruptly dissipates. I'm still not quite sure which of our friends shared his thoughts on appropriate zombie self-defense, but the fact that Brandon agrees with him creates an immediate mood shift.

Nora scrunches up her nose in disgust, wincing slightly.

"What?" Brandon blurts, confused.

Jason takes a beat, recalibrating his approach. "Tell you what," he finally offers. "If you can think of a *good* plan that doesn't involve any bloodshed, we'll try it out. If things go sideways, though, all bets are off. Some zombied-out straight guy's not turning me into a modern-art piece."

"Deal," I reply.

Jason takes note of my relief, smirking. "Don't relax too much; you still need to think of a plan."

"We just need a distraction," I reply. "If we can draw them out of the house long enough, then we can hop down and make a run for Brandon's truck."

"I might have an idea," Hazel suddenly announces.

5

The five of us peer down over the edge of the loft, waiting patiently for our chance to move. It's a tense moment, only elevated by the fact that our ladder has found itself as the centerpiece for the artist's second creation.

The wooden rungs have been sawed in half, separating each side of this tool and creating two even rows of vertical spikes. Various organs that once belonged to Ricky have been violently punctured onto each one, a simple arrangement of deconstructed anatomy.

Suffice to say, we won't be getting back up here once we've made our move.

A loud bang suddenly erupts through the cabin, causing the five of us survivors to flinch in shock. Smoke rises from the barrel of Jason's rifle as the little boy holding it barely reacts. He's accidently fired through a bedroom wall.

The artist notices and begins to laugh, quietly at first, and then gradually transforming into a strange series of guttural screams. Soon enough, the whole family has joined in to create a horrific choir, shrieking wildly for a bit before quieting down and returning to their business.

My heart was already slamming within my chest, but now it's hammering so hard I'm worried the thing's gonna pop.

"Everyone ready?" Hazel questions.

We're too focused to respond, but this plan is going forward regardless of any objections. It's now or never.

A familiar hum suddenly erupts from the back bedroom, causing my muscles to tighten. The buzz shifts a bit, then grows louder and louder as Hazel's drone enters the living room.

The sound is even more obnoxious than I remember, and for a moment I'm overcome with sweet relief.

This is actually going to work, I think to myself.

I glance at Hazel, who's deeply focused on her phone and the attached controller. The last thing I want to do is distract her and send our robot helper careening into a wall, but I also have an outsider's view of just how low it's hovering.

"Give it a little lift," I whisper.

Hazel says nothing in response, but as I glance back over the ledge I notice the drone rising a few feet. It's not entirely out of swatting range for these crazed straights, but it's much better than before.

The zombie family have halted their bizarre, spastic routines and are now gazing at the drone, watching in slack-jawed wonder in the presence of this unknown visitor.

STRAIGHT

"They see it," I hiss. "Get out of there!"

Hazel immediately pilots her drone away from the family. She heads for the open door, making her way out into the cool night air of the desert.

Unfortunately, the curiosity of the overwhelmed doesn't seem to extend much further than their initial glance. All four of them hesitate a moment, swaying from side to side before letting out a few awkward shrieks and returning to their business.

The artist has broken ground on his third sculpture, but his wife has removed Ricky's arm from the first construction. She's attempting to boil it on the stove.

Unfortunately, the zombie housewife finds plenty of trouble fitting this limb into her pot without the whole thing tipping over and spilling across the range, but that hasn't stopped her from trying.

Meanwhile, the children are standing across from one another, staring daggers at their sibling as they take turns roughly shoving their opponent's shoulder and emitting a strange gurgling sound.

"Well, that sure as hell didn't work," Brandon blurts.

I'd love any reason to turn and unload on the guy, but he's right.

We hoped the drone might coax them off into the desert with its mysterious buzz, but it appears these peculiar hobbies are much more important to the overwhelmed.

Finally, Hazel lets out a long sigh and pilots her drone back inside. She floats it up to join us in the loft, then lands the device and shuts it down.

"We just need something that'll grab their attention

better," I offer. "This can still work."

"One of you could hop down there and start running," Brandon suggests.

"Are you volunteering?" Jason counters. "Don't forget, daddy's after you, too."

Nora reaches out and pats the little drone on what you might consider its robot head. "It's too bad this little rascal isn't gay. They'd be all over it."

Suddenly, Hazel's eyes go wide. "The overwhelmed can sense some kind of biological queerness," she blurts, hurrying over to Nora, "that's how they separate us from the larger population. The thing is, there's also evidence that social cues can play a role in their hunting patterns."

"Like what?" I question.

"All kinds of things," Hazel continues, then motions toward her girlfriend. "Give me your bra."

Nora is deeply confused by this request, but she trusts Hazel and doesn't hesitate while reaching under her shirt to remove it. She extracts a light-gray bra with a vibrant, rainbow-colored elastic band from her sleeve and hands it over.

"Thank you," Hazel continues. "I've been thinking about this ever since the artist got fixated on Brandon after their scuffle. That particular overwhelmed isn't looking for *revenge;* he's just tracking Brandon as queer because he helped us."

"I ain't queer," Brandon interjects.

"Thank fuck," I blurt.

There's a loud rip as Hazel begins to tear the circular elastic band away from Nora's bra, an unexpected maneuver that causes Nora to cry out in surprise.

STRAIGHT

"Hey! That was expensive!" Nora erupts.

For the first time, Hazel's focus is actually broken. She turns to Nora and gives her a quick kiss. "I'm sorry," she offers.

Once the elastic band is free, Hazel takes it over to her drone and begins wrapping it around the device. "Who has music on their phone?"

"I do," I volunteer. "We can stream anything you want."

Hazel shakes her head. "It needs to be downloaded already. No service, remember?"

We all exchange glances, coming up empty until, finally, Jason takes a deep breath and regrettably hands over his phone. "I've got some stuff on here."

Hazel takes the device skeptically. "I don't think you're gonna have the kind of thing we're looking for," she replies, quickly opening an app and strolling through Jason's saved songs.

She gets a few swipes down and then stops abruptly, glancing up at Jason with a knowing grin.

***

The drone creeps back over the ledge, hovering high as Hazel takes a minute to understand its awkward new weight distribution. Fortunately, this song has an intro, but there's not much time before the beat kicks in.

The family glances up, and while they'd previously gone back to their work, they've clearly noticed something is a little different this time around. The rainbow elastic band certainly gives our little device some Pride flag pop, and the phone strapped to its back has altered the shape slightly.

The artist staggers forward a bit, his mouth opening and closing in abrupt snaps. He lets out a single, powerful shriek, then jaunts a few steps closer.

"Go, go, go!" I command. "They're tracking it."

Hazel drops her drone a smidge more, focused on clearing the doorframe on her way outside. This is a necessary move, but at this height it would be *so* easy for any member of our little zombie family to reach out and smack it down.

Suddenly, the intro ends and the song begins.

"You better *work!*" RuPaul's voice rings out, a throbbing, constant beat dropping and the familiar keyboards of *Supermodel* ringing out through the cabin.

All four of the overwhelmed spring into action, lurching toward the drone as they howl with unbridled rage.

"Now!" I cry.

Hazel slams the joystick of her controller down, shooting her vehicle forward as the artist takes a swing with his now-buzzing handsaw. He's inches away from the delicate blades of the drone, the mere air displacement of his swipe causing Hazel's hovercraft to rock from side to side.

Fortunately, she's a hell of a pilot, and seconds later her drone is escaping into the darkness of the desert.

"You better work! Cover Girl! Work it girl! Give a twirl! Do your thing!" RuPaul's voice cries out from Jason's phone with joyful exuberance, echoing through the vast Joshua Tree desert.

The zombie family immediately springs into action,

sprinting after Hazel's drone in a shrieking mob. We hesitate no more than three seconds after they've left the cabin before dropping down and springing into action.

Our crew filters out the front door as Hazel continues to pilot her drone in the exact opposite direction, leading the straights off into the desert brambles. Hazel is slower than the rest, deeply focused on her job as a pilot, so we pull back as we begin our trek up the hillside road.

Brandon has taken the lead, baseball bat held tight as we push onward to his truck. "It's right over here," he hisses in a low tone.

The incredible beauty of our surroundings is almost comical in juxtaposition to the horrific events of this evening. While a blanket of stars twinkles across the sky above like mesmerizing cosmic glitter, utter chaos unfolds down here on Earth.

My eyes have just barely adjusted to this vast darkness when Brandon's vehicle comes into view; a large, dark shape parked next to an even bigger looming boulder.

There's a faint jingle as Brandon pulls the keys from his pocket, approaching his truck.

Suddenly, a pair of brilliant headlights illuminate the scene, blasting to life before us and causing our ragtag gang of companions to immediately shield our eyes. The change is so abrupt that I stumble a bit, struggling to regain my footing on this bumpy dirt road.

"Oh fuck," Hazel blurts, dropping her phone.

She scrambles to pick it up, but it's already too late. The drone has crashed.

Before us, a rusty metal door creaks open and a figure steps down from their imposing automobile. What first appeared to be desert boulders is actually a massive truck.

"Who's that?" Brandon calls out, his hand over his eyes as he creeps toward the high beams.

"Need a lift?" the silhouetted figure calls over, sounding vaguely normal. "Looks like you're stuck. Toast in the morning. Hairless. Ohio. Paste."

Brandon glances over at his own ride, then back to the figure, blatantly ignoring the awkward parts of that introduction. "No, I'm not stuck," he yells. "We're fine."

It's only then I notice the massive orange letters plastered across the side of this unexpected vehicle. YUCCA VALLEY TOWING, it reads. A monstrous set of chains have been wrapped around Brandon's bumper, holding his vehicle in place.

The tow truck driver steps forward, now close enough for Brandon to realize the man's completely naked other than the cap perched atop his head. He's gripping a tire iron in his hand.

"*We're* fine? Who's we?" the driver questions. "Over easy!"

"I don't... I'm sorry," Brandon stammers, struggling to stay focused despite the stark naked man settled directly before him. The nudity has made Brandon deeply uncomfortable, barely able to form a coherent thought. "It's just me out here."

The rest of us start backing away slowly, putting even more space between us and our straight companion.

"Who is we? Who is we?" the driver demands to know. He repeats this question again and again, his voice mutating slightly with every repetition as he grows increasingly livid. "Who is we? Who is we?"

Soon enough, the driver is screaming at the top of his lungs, yelling in Brandon's face.

Jason leans toward me, his voice hushed as he makes the call. "Sorry buddy, this is where your plan ends and mine begins." He leans down and picks up an enormous rock, preparing to spring into action.

Just then, however, two more figures emerge from the tow truck. It's the man and woman we'd seen standing beside their flaming car on the way in. They're just as nude as before, only now they're absolutely drenched in fresh blood. The woman is holding a chainsaw, while her companion drags a sledgehammer behind him.

"Plan C. We've gotta go," I blurt, retreating even faster now. "Back to the other car!"

As the chainsaw roars to life we spring into action, the whole gang turning and sprinting back around the hillside bend in the light of the tow truck's high beams. I'm running as fast as I can, but it's difficult to see the ground amid this chaos. My ankles are twisting and turning as I struggle to find any footing atop these awkward desert rocks.

Of course, we're not *all* running away.

Refusing to select from the options of fight or flight, Brandon has decided to do nothing at all. He stands with a shocked look on his face, watching as the overwhelmed push past him and follow us down the hill.

Meanwhile, the original family we'd been so careful to avoid can be heard shrieking in the darkness, making their way back toward us in a state of belligerent rage.

I use every ounce of strength I can muster to

propel myself onward, the lights of the cabin growing larger and larger with every step I take. I can see Jason's car sitting right there next to it, and while there's not enough gas in the tank to get very far, it's still plenty to save us from imminent death.

Glancing over my shoulder, I notice we're actually pulling ahead, putting more and more distance between us and our pursuers who've just barely made it around the bend with their heavy weaponry.

My excitement immediately falters, however, when Jason takes a fatal misstep.

Through pure chance, my friend's foot lands in one of the many large holes and awkward grades that cover this unkept dirt road. His ankle twists hard as an audible pop rings out, causing a look of excruciating pain to erupt across his face. Jason slams hard onto the ground, completely knocking the wind out of his large frame.

Nora and Hazel don't even notice, still running ahead, but I immediately skid to a stop. I turn back to see our pursuers gaining on Jason as he struggles to stand and hobble onward. He's not nearly quick enough to escape now.

Our gazes meet. Deep down we both know he's fucked, but I don't care. I start doubling back for my friend, but he shakes his head and calls out to stop me.

Jason reaches into his pocket, finding his car keys and quickly pulling them forth. With the flick of his wrist, he tosses them over to me.

"Go!" he commands. "Get them out of here."

"Fuck that," I reply. I catch his keys but continue up the road in an attempt to help my friend.

"Run!" Jason cries. "Get everyone somewhere safe!"

The three pursuers are right behind him now, their weapons raised and their eyes filled with a haunting look of rage and excitement. They're angry, that's for sure, but they still maintain those bizarre smiles from ear to ear.

Jason's right, I suddenly realize. There's nothing I can do.

Before I have the chance to even try, however, Jason takes matters into his own hands. He hobbles to the edge of the road, gazing down at the rocky embankment below. The slope of the hillside is the steepest at this point, and the trip down would be incredibly unpleasant.

Still, it's faster than he's moving currently.

"It don't matter what you wear, they're checking out your savoir faire," Jason sings, drawing the group's attention, "and it don't matter what you do, cause everything looks good on you!"

Seconds before the gang reaches Jason, he hurls himself over the edge of the hillside, tumbling end over end down the rocky, dusty slope and into the darkness below.

"Wait!" I cry out, knowing it's much too late but the word forcing its way from my mouth regardless, an untethered expression of deep anguish.

The three pursuers stop, hesitating for a moment as they stare at me and consider their options. Seconds later, they turn and start climbing down the hillside after Jason. They scream and howl, their voices ringing out through the night.

I'm sick with anger and frustration, and part of me wants to collapse into a blubbering heap right here and now. Unfortunately, I don't have that luxury.

I turn and continue sprinting back toward Jason's car. The ladies are way ahead of me, frantically pacing back and forth as they wait for my arrival.

"I'm coming! I'm coming!" I cry, hustling down the dirt road.

I can hear the shrieks and howls of the family growing louder as they make their return, but the vastness of this wide-open landscape and the anxiety that bubbles through my nervous system makes it difficult to tell where their cries are emanating from. Regardless of the source, our solution remains the same: We need to get the hell out of here.

I'm running so fast that I slide across the dirt in an attempt to stop myself. I swiftly pull back and grip the door handle, using it to center my weight as I shove in the key and unlock the vehicle. The three of us dive inside and I start the ignition, the car roaring to life.

Suddenly, one of the doors flies open causing all three of us to scream in alarm. I glance over my shoulder to see Brandon jump inside and slam the door behind him, a horrified look contorting his face.

"Go! Go! Go!" he screams.

The artist is sprinting toward us now, his eyes dead-set on Brandon as he hoists the battery-powered saw above his head and lets out an animalistic scream.

I throw the car into drive and hit the gas, causing us to shoot forward at such high velocity that my skull pulls back against the headrest behind me. I crank the wheel hard, throwing up dirt and rocks in a massive plume as the vehicle makes a half-rotation and rockets up the road.

STRAIGHT

The artist is now in the beam of my headlights.

We're flying at incredible speeds, so I find myself with no more than a split second of reaction time. I'm exhausted, panicked, and furiously angry, and this cocktail of emotions swirls together to create something absolutely vicious. A part of me wants so badly to slam into him and laugh as he flips over the hood, to break every bone in his body.

Yet, at the last second, I swerve. The car careens around the artist, who begins to frantically run after us with his saw held high. "Four hundred dollars! Four hundred dollars! Four hundred dollars!" he's shrieking for reasons I can't even begin to comprehend.

We shoot up the dirt road, the entire car trembling so hard I'd swear it's gonna fall apart at any second. As I reach the ridge, however, I slam on my brakes.

"What the hell are you doing?" Nora screams.

I roll down the window and gaze over the edge where Jason disappeared. "Jason!" I cry out, my voice carrying through the empty desert.

The expressions of Nora and Hazel suddenly falter as they realize our tight-knit crew is missing one very important piece.

"Where is he?" Nora erupts.

"I don't—I don't know," I stammer frantically. "He's down there somewhere."

I glance in my rearview mirror as the artist continues his frantic approach.

Suddenly, the back window shatters as a rifle blast erupts through the air. Nora and Hazel duck for cover, glass raining down and catching in their hair while Brandon and I jump in shock. Fortunately, this treated safety pane won't cut anyone, but I'm more concerned about the bullet passing through it.

I now notice the overwhelmed boy is stumbling up the road after his father, his rickety walk almost comical if not for the fact that he's carelessly swinging a hunting rifle from side to side as he goes.

Meanwhile, the artist has almost reached us.

It feels as though my heart is being torn from my chest as I slam the gas pedal again, rumbling down the dirt road while tears fill my eyes. There's no question Jason wanted us to keep going. He knew the longer we stayed back at the cabin, the more our chances of survival would plummet.

But it still kills me.

As we continue onward, the dirt road eventually transforms into crumbling, neglected pavement. Brandon is absolutely ecstatic, adrenaline pouring out of him as he punches the ceiling and lets out a series of excited whoops, thankful to be alive. Hazel, Nora and I are thankful too, but our mood is much more subdued. Nobody says a word, staring out at the desolate road before us.

Eventually, I slow the vehicle and turn off my headlights. We crawl along in the darkness.

6

Our steady pace leaves plenty of time to observe the awkward shifts in this once-familiar landscape. Every so often we'll notice something odd, evidence of someone else's horrifying story that we're only a tangential part of.

We watch as headlights rumble through the distance, circling a few times before taking off along a dangerously sidewinding path.

Gunshots and screams ring out sporadically, a faint sense of alarm filling the darkness and then dissipating just as quickly as it arrived.

The silence in this car is overwhelming, but necessary. In a practical sense, it's deathly important the four of us avoid detection out here in the middle of nowhere, rolling along over cracked, sand-covered pavement while we struggle to catch our breath and find our bearings.

The quiet is more than just a survival technique, however—it's a moment of emotional processing. While

Brandon seems to be doing just fine, especially given the circumstances, the rest of us are still reeling from losing our friend.

The most frustrating part is that nobody actually saw it happen. For all we know, Jason could still be out there, tucked under a giant boulder as he waits out the evening on his own.

The idea is thrilling, and the unfiltered hope that surges through my body when the concept crosses my mind is intoxicating. It's such a nice thought that I can't help but find myself drawn deeper and deeper into it, considering the option of turning this car back around and conducting an incredibly dangerous search-and-rescue mission.

This is when I have to pull back and get my head on straight, when I have to accept that returning to the cabin is a death wish. Jason is gone, but I know exactly what he'd do if he was here.

He'd tell me to keep going, to drive as far away from that place as possible. If I doubled back at this point, he'd be tearing out his hair in frustration. Despite my gnawing ache to turn around, it's this knowledge of my late friend's wishes that keeps me pushing onward.

I glance in the rearview mirror, my gaze drifting from Hazel to Nora as they stare quietly from opposing windows. A look at their body language might cause any casual observer to assume they're disconnecting in this moment of hardship and trauma, but noticing the seat between them tells another story. They hold hands, fingers woven together in unity.

"We're gonna need to park somewhere and wait it out," I finally announce.

STRAIGHT

The car stays quiet a little longer as everyone sits with this news, not exactly thrilled by the only option we have. It's not the worst plan, a way of doubling down on the idea we'd already been employing, but it's also tough not to feel like sitting ducks out here.

Who really knows how much the overwhelmed can sense us? How powerful this belligerent, rage-filled gaydar really is?

On one hand, the artist could've made his way down to our cabin thanks to the racket Brandon and Ricky were making with their stupid little prank, but he got there pretty quickly. Maybe he was already on the way, some undiscovered pheromones drifting off our bodies and leading the artist directly to our location.

Regardless, hunkering down and staying quiet is the only choice we've been given. We'll run out of gas soon enough.

"Wait it out?" Brandon questions, turning to offer a look of confusion. "I thought you just needed a car to get to Palm Springs. We're in it."

"A car that's not running on fumes," I retort. "The stations are all closed and everyone's locked down. Maybe we could siphon off some fuel from a parked car, but we don't have the tools for that."

"I know where we could get some gas," Brandon states.

I glance over, certain he's messing with me, but Brandon remains straight-faced.

"Wait, really?" I question. "Where?"

"At the saloon," he continues. "It's stored way in the back, but it's there. We get so many folks hiking over to

Bobcat's after their car kicked the bucket that we figured we should just keep some fuel around."

"Are we close?" I ask.

Brandon nods. "Right up there," he replies, pointing to a turnoff in the road that snakes its way over a nearby ridge.

I follow his directions.

Soon enough, we're creeping our way up this twisting road, slipping between a canyon of rocky crags in the darkness. Our headlights still off, it's difficult to make out more than a few shadows in the luminescent moonlight above. I barely notice an overturned semi-truck on the side of the road, the rectangular behemoth looming tall as it rests on its side.

I lean forward, gazing up at the vehicle as we slowly pass, watching in awe like I'm witnessing a living dinosaur under the silver moonlight. I'm confused why a scarecrow is positioned next to the vehicle's cab, a truly random pairing of unrelated objects, but it quickly dawns on me that this could actually be a human body on a pike.

Without the help of sunlight, I'll never know, and I think it'd rather not.

Meanwhile, Jason's car is beginning to sputter and rattle even more as it desperately sucks down fumes, prompting a surge of fear as we push onward.

Thankfully, we soon emerge on the other side of the canyon, finding ourselves on a flat desert plane once again. To the left is a small community of bungalows and trailers, their lights turned off as they look down on us like empty skulls. To the right is the familiar sight of Pioneertown.

STRAIGHT

Unlike the rest of the desert, these structures are dimly illuminated in the evening, faint bulbs casting the scene with shadowy menace from the ground up.

"Okay, let's keep it slow up here," Brandon warns. "My boss doesn't believe in the vaccine. Hank just goes to bed early and hopes to sleep through it. Can't kill anyone if you're not awake."

I glance over at Brandon, raising an eyebrow in bewildered amusement. "Glad to know the rest of the world is pinning our survival on their sleep schedule."

Brandon says nothing in return, just points toward a building at this distant edge of Pioneertown. "Park around the other side," he instructs. "It's better to walk instead of rolling up to the saloon over all that gravel. We'll be fine as long as Hank doesn't wake up."

I stop where I'm instructed.

"Who's going?" Brandon questions, glancing around the car.

I can't help but scoff. "Are you kidding me? *You're* going."

Our incredibly frustrating companion shakes his head. "No way, I did my part. I got you here, now you fetch the fuel."

I just stare at him, dumbfounded by the man's utter selfishness.

"What?" Brandon continues. "Seems fair to me."

Finally Nora pipes up from the back seat. "They're not after you, you dumb fuck. You can just *walk in there* and get the fuel."

Brandon turns in his seat, getting defensive now. "Hey! That guy with the face paint tried to kill me. He's probably trudging across the desert right now with that buzz saw. And besides, Ricky was as straight as they come. Look what happened to him!"

Nora and I exchange glances.

Hazel, who's been gazing out the window and tracking the desert for any movement, finally adds her voice. "Typical ally," is all she says.

Brandon looks confused. "Hey, I'm not homophobic or whatever. I don't care what y'all do. I *am* an ally."

"Until it gets difficult," Hazel replies, finally turning her gaze and pointing it directly at him. "Until it gets dangerous."

"It's been dangerous this whole damn time," Brandon counters.

"You mean over the last few hours?" Hazel counters. "Or over the last two years since The Blank Space appeared? Or maybe you mean the decades of unnecessary and deeply harmful conversion therapy? Or the centuries of bigotry and violence? As an ally, you were part of fighting that, too, right?"

"I wasn't around for that," Brandon counters.

"You were around for some of it," Hazel retorts. "What did you do to help?"

Brandon is silent for a moment, taking it in.

"When it's time to put *your* neck out for us, are you gonna help? Or are you gonna turn and run?" she questions.

"I already *did* help," Brandon erupts, growing even more flustered.

"You took a swing before you knew it would put

STRAIGHT

you in danger," Hazel explains. "It's easy to be an ally when you don't have to give anything up. You can talk and talk and talk all day, and get plenty of credit for your words. I'm not speaking on that. What I said was, 'when it's time to put your *neck* out.' What are you gonna do when the guillotine is sitting right there and your friends are lying under it? Are you gonna join that fight?"

Brandon is silent. He stays put.

Nora's had enough. "Just go get the fucking fuel you dick! The zombies are after us, not you!"

Finally, Brandon lets out a frustrated grunt. He opens the car door and climbs out, then quietly creeps off into the night.

Nora shrugs. "Sometimes you've just gotta yell."

The three of us settle back into our seats as we wait, but we're certainly not relaxed. From here we can't see the campy old west facades of Pioneertown, as we're tucked around the side of this building, but I keep my eyes trained on the nearby corner for any sign of movement. I crack the windows a bit, eavesdropping on the magnificent silence of the desert around us.

As I sit and listen, I can't help letting my thoughts drift back to Jason, wondering where he is right now and struggling to accept my responsibility in how he got there. I picture the rocky hillside he tumbled over, his mangled, twisted body laying sprawled out at the bottom as those three frightening attackers stand over him.

I wonder if I'll ever know what happened, if there'll be a trace of him left when Saturation Day is over.

These thoughts consume me, flooding my mind and causing a dreadful sickness to creep into the pit of my stomach.

"He's not coming back," Nora states coldly.

I blink twice, pulled back into reality by the sound of her voice. I now realize I've been lost in thought for quite a while, the seconds turning into minutes turning into… I'm not quite sure.

"How long has it been?" I question.

"Half hour" she replies.

Longer than I expected, and certainly long enough to be worried about where the hell Brandon ran off to. While I suppose it's entirely possible the artist has followed us all the way here and finally taken his revenge, that outcome seems very, very unlikely. What's more probable is that Brandon decided to split and left us to fend for ourselves.

It suddenly crosses my mind that this gas tank in the back of the saloon might be nothing more than a fabrication, a way for Brandon to catch a ride home and nothing more.

"I'm going in," I announce.

"Wait, what?" Nora blurts. "No!"

"Are we trying to get to Palm Springs or what?" I continue.

Nora has no response for this, realizing that, despite her initial objection, I'm right. We can't just sit here all night. Besides, even if we *did* hide in the darkness, the effects of The Blank Space won't end until late tomorrow afternoon.

In broad daylight we'd be sitting ducks.

"He's right," Hazel finally chimes in to confirm.

"All three of us don't need to put ourselves in

danger," I continue. "I'll look for the gas tank, and if I don't find anything I'll come right back so we can figure out a new plan. If you have any problems, there's probably enough fumes left to get out of here."

"And… leave you behind?" Nora questions, racked with emotion.

"Fuck no," I retort. "Circle back for me; I'm not that much of a hero."

I toss them the keys, then quietly open the car door. I creep out into the cool evening air, standing up and hustling over to the edge of the building we've cloaked ourselves behind. With my heart slamming in my chest, I peer out from behind the edge to take in this strange, surreal main street. My destination sits quiet and dark at the far end.

Pioneertown is impressively detailed, each and every one of the structures immaculately constructed for an immersive aesthetic. Most of these structures are connected within, running the length of the street and featuring a variety of designations, from bath house to bank to brothel.

Rarely do they actually offer the service listed out front. Instead, these structures provide visitors with what amounts to a few long, drawn out gift shops, a place to buy candy or crystals or hats with the words JOSHUA TREE NATIONAL PARK embroidered across the front.

Since I'm hoping to stay quiet and undetected, the best way of making my way to the saloon would be to creep along within these structures. Unfortunately, they're closed for the evening, but the wooden overhangs that run along the storefronts do a good enough job of keeping me hidden.

I tread lightly over the planks that make up these old west sidewalks, trying my best to avoid any creaks.

As I pass the gallows, I gaze up in slight amazement at the audacity of this looming display. While public hangings are certainly a real part of humanity's past, you rarely witness them fully embraced in these present day recreations. I've seen plenty of local amusement parks manifest a similar time period without these massive execution instruments.

Not in Pioneertown.

The structure itself is simple enough, a square wooden platform some seven feet up that features a line of wide open trap doors. There's a staircase leading up to this level, and it's here that three nooses dangle from an even higher rung. They sway and turn in the wind, ready for imaginary frontier justice.

I try my best to ignore this foreboding symbol of death, but it's difficult to pretend I didn't just walk by a blatant warning sign, an expression of what fate has in store for me.

I shake my head, brushing it off before glancing down and discovering I've arrived at a small faux graveyard. A taxidermied raven stares blankly from atop one of the many wooden crosses that dot these grounds at various haphazard angles.

Creeping onward, I finally arrive at the side door of Bobcat's Saloon.

According to Brandon, the gas can is located in a storage room at the back of the main dining area, and I use my earlier patronage as a way to find my bearings. I can remember two distinct doors on the far wall, and I've gotta imagine one of them will take me where I need to go.

In and out quick, I remind myself.

I check the back entrance to find that it is, in fact, unlocked, then I slip inside. The air around me immediately changes, warm and filled with the scent of stale beer and good food. It'd be quite welcoming in another circumstance, but right now it sends a chill down my spine. It feels like a crowd, and right now a crowd is the last thing I need.

The main lighting fixtures are switched off, but there's illumination behind the bar and a few lamps turned on in the dining area beyond, casting the scene in an assortment of long, angular shadows. I glance around the room, constantly detecting signs of life before realizing my eyes are playing tricks on me.

I'm on edge.

Still, I need to stay vigilant. Brandon told me flatly that the owner, Hank, wasn't vaccinated, and that he's tucked away in some back-room living quarters.

At least, I hope he's tucked away.

I slip deeper into the building, making my way through the darkness. I check every wooden floorboard with my weight before moving onward, noting even the simplest noises as they fill this otherwise quiet space.

This level of care takes some time, but eventually I arrive at the dining room. Here, I'm faced with the two doors I remember, a distinct choice with potentially vast consequences. It's a coin flip what could lie beyond, and the owner's living area seems like a perfectly reasonable bet for either.

I take my chances, randomly selecting the frame on

the right and then slinking through the darkness toward it. I weave my way around these empty tables, my breathing slow and purposeful as I focus on my mission. Above me, huge taxidermied animals gaze down with their vacant marble eyes, including the enormous centerpiece of a stoic buffalo.

The beast watches closely, seemingly aware that I could end up like him at any moment, stuffed and mounted.

I reach the door and carefully pull it open, finding myself in a pitch-black hallway. While there'd been just enough dim light in the saloon's main areas to carve a path, that's no longer possible.

Fortunately, I've got my cell phone handy, and while the service might be shot, it still makes for a pretty good flashlight. I pull forth this tiny device and pop it on as a burst of illumination floods the hallway. It's a short, compact space with a door at either end, but in this moment the only detail that matters is the figure crouched in the corner.

I let out a startled gasp, stumbling as I back away. The figure rises and rushes toward me, but before things get out of hand I hear them hissing my name.

"Isaac! It's me! It's me!" the silhouette reveals.

Relief pumps through me as I recognize Brandon's familiar tone. "Oh my fucking god," I sigh. "What are you doing?"

"What do you mean?" he whispers. "I'm getting the gas can!"

"You're taking forever!" I blurt.

Brandon shakes his head in frustration. "Well, I'm *so sorry* I'm not saving you from the zombie apocalypse fast enough. The keys to this room are usually hanging behind the bar."

"But you found them?" I continue, recognizing the longer we stand here the more dangerous it becomes.

Brandon nods. "I just can't remember which key it is and I didn't wanna turn on the lights."

My companion motions for me to follow, ducking back into the hallway and making our way to the door in question. With the help of my phone's flashlight, Brandon can easily sort through his key ring and find the instrument he's looking for. He slips it into the lock and soon enough we're pushing through into the storage area.

The room is packed full of strange objects and canned rations, a mix between a test kitchen and a funky antique shop. Fully stocked shelves of beans and tomato sauce line one wall, and a massive, broken neon sign rests against the other.

I keep my eyes peeled, holding the light for Brandon to see as he rummages around. He's being a little louder than I'd prefer, but fortunately the search doesn't last long. Soon enough, Brandon is hurrying back toward me with his baseball bat in one hand and a large plastic jug of gasoline in the other.

"Let's go," he offers confidently.

I turn off the flashlight and pivot to lead us back, heading down the hallway and out into the dining room where I stop in my tracks.

A figure stands in the middle of the tables, facing away from us and staring at the wall in a rigid, trancelike state. Even in this dim lighting, I can still make out the glint of a large knife in his hand.

Brandon runs directly into my back, causing a loud burst of air to escape his lips. Annoyed, he lets the beginning of a word slip out before catching sight of our new friend, then quickly falls into silence.

Frozen solid, the two of us wait for any kind of movement as our breath remains caught in our throats. My eyes are fixed squarely on the man before me, who I now recognize as the bartender and owner, Hank.

I start backing away, moving down the hall one step, then another, then another.

A strangled yelp suddenly erupts from the owner's throat, causing me to jump in surprise, but the man doesn't move. Seconds later, another scream fills the room, an expression of rage with no direction to go but outward.

Once we've ducked back around the corner, Brandon nods toward the second door in this hallway. I fall into step behind him as the two of us creep along, making our way through a dimly lit kitchen and then onward to the back exit.

Soon enough, we're emerging into the cool night air of the desert once again, relief building with every passing step that puts a little more distance between us and the knife wielding howler.

This is a hell of a situation I've found myself in, and Jason's tragic end still hangs over me like a specter, but as Brandon and I creep our way through Pioneertown I can't help the potent sense of optimism that floods my veins. Throughout the night many obstacles have been thrown in our way, and one by one we've knocked them down by working together and having each other's backs.

Even this fucking asshole to my left.

STRAIGHT

Smiling, I glance over at Brandon to discover he's disappeared.

I stop abruptly, scanning the artificial frontier landscape for any signs of life.

"Hey!" I call out in a strained half-whisper. "Brandon?"

If he wasn't carrying the gasoline can I'd consider just barreling onward, but at this point I've found myself in a particularly dangerous situation with nothing to show for it.

My gaze drifts from the gallows, to the old graveyard, to an enormous aloe plant that erupts from the ground in a bouquet of mint green, succulent spines. It's in this final location I spot Brandon, his eyes wide and his finger pressed firmly to his lips in an expression that could only be interpreted as *shut the fuck up*. He's crouched behind the plant, hidden away in the darkness.

The second we make eye contact, Brandon nods past me, signaling me to follow his gaze.

I do as instructed, my line of sight drifting to a shadowy overhang where it comes to rest on a figure shuffling about. I recognize this man immediately, recalling the way he'd been sauntering through the saloon when we first arrived in Joshua Tree. The cowboy hat is still perched atop his head, and the dusty boots remain firmly planted upon his feet. A huge bundle of rope has been wrapped around the cowboy's shoulder, tied off in what looks like the knot of a simple lasso.

The biggest change, however, is the old six-shooter that once hung behind the bar. It now dangles from a loose belt around the man's waist.

The cowboy is mumbling something to himself as he blunders through the darkness with an exaggerated, straight-legged walk, spitting and frothing at the mouth in simmering indignation.

He hasn't noticed me yet, but he's headed this way.

Thinking fast, I duck into a nearby building labeled GENERAL STORE. There's no door on the structure, which is the only reason it's currently open, and instead of commercial goods it offers a few informative pamphlets detailing Pioneertown's history.

I crouch down, holding my breath and pressing myself against the inside wall as the cowboy's footsteps grow louder and louder upon the nearby wooden sidewalk.

Eventually, he stops.

"You've been among the willows for too long!" he screams, his voice strained and gargling. "Time for me to take ya' in, partner! Dead or alive!"

I freeze, terrified I've been discovered before slowly realizing these are just the ravings of a madman. The cowboy has no idea I'm here, simply expressing a deep frustration as it bubbles up from the pit of his subconscious mind.

"There's gold in them hills!" he shrieks, his voice erupting in a high pitched squeal that echoes through the vacant structures of Pioneertown.

The cowboy takes a few more steps, close enough for me to detect the faint jangle of spurs. He's fully committed to this delusion.

I now realize I haven't let out a single breath since ducking into the shadows, and my lungs are starting to burn. I desperately want to exhale, but at this point even the faintest movement could give me up.

Finally, the cowboy continues onward, stomping away over the wooden sidewalk and allowing me the sweet relief of exhalation. I take a moment to collect myself, listening intently until I'm certain the coast is clear before climbing to my feet. I gaze out from the windows of this small building, examining my surroundings.

Brandon has disappeared, no longer behind the enormous aloe plant.

Good, I think. He should be getting that gasoline back to the car as quickly as possible.

I step out from the general store and continue down this rustic dirt avenue, sticking to the shadows. I don't get far, however.

"Yee-ha!" comes an exuberant shriek from behind me.

There's a loud crack as pain explodes through my skull, radiating from the back of my head and spreading in a blinding cascade. I stumble forward, struggling to turn and defend myself when I'm struck for a second time.

I realize it's the butt of his gun as my face slams the dirt and the taste of dust and rocks floods my bloody mouth. Warm liquid runs through my hair, freshly sprung from two new dents in my skull.

"Dead or alive or dead or alive or dead!" the cowboy screams excitedly.

7

I try once more to get up, but in this upside down, discombobulated moment I'm quickly learning just how hard I've been hit. My whole equilibrium is off, causing even the simplest bodily commands to acquire a Herculean level of difficulty. Simply putting my hand against the dirt and pushing myself upward becomes damn near impossible.

Still, I give it my best shot, and for the second time I end up collapsing to the ground in a coughing, sputtering mess.

I can feel the cowboy stepping over me, the weight of his lasso coiling around my body as he unravels it gleefully. Seconds later, the harshness of the rope pulls roughly across my face, tightening unexpectedly around my neck.

Wide eyed, I let out a final gasp as my windpipe is shut tight. I'm yanked back, pulled across the rough ground as my hands frantically tug at the noose.

While the cowboy and I are similar in stature, I'm

no match for his adrenaline fueled wrath as he yanks me along in a crawling, sputtering mess.

"Dead or alive or dead or alive!" the overwhelmed maniac keeps screaming, the words tumbling out of his mouth in a terrifying cackle.

I've lost track of my bearings, but quickly discover my position as we reach the steps of the gallows. Immediately, a second rush of survival instinct pulses through my body in a wave. I pull back on the rope and struggle to turn away, but a third strike from the butt of the cowboy's gun nearly renders me unconscious.

My body is limp, like a fighter ready to tap out, and I feel as though I'm watching my battered and bruised frame from the outside looking in. The cowboy throws his rope over the central bar of the gallows, a brand new noose to go along with the previous offerings. I'm forced to stand straight up as he pulls it taut, struggling for air as I sway back and forth on my tiptoes.

I'm vaguely aware just how close I am to one of the square holes in this wooden platform, dancing around the edge and doing everything I can to keep from falling in.

I consider putting all my energy into one last swing at the cowboy, but at this point a miss would send me plummeting, the noose tightening from the force of my own bodyweight.

Gallows work the best with a sudden jerk rather than a faint slip. Without the traditional trapdoor plunge, and plenty of slack to go with it, my neck likely won't snap.

My eyes go even wider as this thought consumes my mind. Always the optimist, I'd been considering this potential drawn out death as an opportunity for escape, but escape is not in the cards.

It'll just be more agonizing.

The cowboy finishes tying off the other end of his lasso and saunters over to me with his strange walk, an otherwise comical approximation of an old west gunslinger turned horrific and strange. He's wearing the same frightening grin most overwhelmed like to sport, a smile so wide it appears to stretch across his entire face. Meanwhile, his eyes are flooded with absolute rage.

At this point, the rope around my neck has pulled so tight that I can't even cry for help. "Please," is all I can manage to say, the single word falling out of me in a broken croak.

"Dead or alive!" the cowboy screams as he glances down at my feet and raises his eyebrows a few times, exaggerating the movement like he's about to tell some hilarious joke.

The cowboy begins to kick at my tip-toed feet, playfully attempting to knock me off balance and send me plummeting through the hole in the gallows. I sway to either side, desperately struggling to get away and finding it more difficult by the second.

"Hey!" a familiar voice suddenly calls out.

I glance at the bottom of the gallows steps to find Brandon, the baseball bat gripped tightly in his hands. The cowboy barely notices, however, ignoring his fellow straight man.

"Hey!" Brandon repeats, marching up the stairs toward us and readying his weapon.

The general criticism of straight allies is that they only show up when it's easy and convenient, and there's a lot of truth to that statement. It doesn't take much to *call* yourself an ally, but will you be there when it actually matters?

While I've had my doubts about Brandon, I'm so damn thankful for the guy as he rushes to my aid.

Just as I think this, however, an earsplitting bang erupts through the night. I'm so startled that I finally lose my footing, slipping into the hole with a sharp tug.

Thankfully, I only drop a foot or so and my neck stays intact for the time being.

I watch as Brandon grabs his arm, then pulls away his hand with a look of shock and horror. He's bleeding from a fresh bullet wound.

The cowboy stands firm between me and my ally, his stance mimicking every old west dual put to film. The cowboy's hand sits inches above his six-shooter, ready to fire off another shot should Brandon try stopping him again.

As I watch Brandon's hesitation, a terrible, sinking realization washes over me. I know exactly what's going to happen well before Brandon takes his first step back and throws his hands up in submission.

Brandon takes one last glance at me, as if to say he's sorry, but after that he simply can't bring himself to look again.

My ally backs all the way down the staircase, then turns and staggers off into the desert.

Meanwhile, I'm pitifully struggling to kick my feet back onto the ledge. For a brief moment I was clawing the rope around my neck, but now I can't even raise my hands that high.

Once Brandon is out of sight, the cowboy leaves me hanging and begins to saunter his way back down the steps. My eyes track him, blurring and fading as the darkness begins to overwhelm my vision.

The cowboy steps out in front of the gallows, watching from the ground as though he's now a captivated audience member. He's still wearing that same horrific smile, still perfectly happy to be snuffing out the life of a fellow human being.

This is it, I suddenly realize. *This is the end, and I'm so fucking angry.*

I'm not exactly sure what I imagined these final moments of life would be like, although I certainly didn't picture hanging from the gallows in a cheesy tourist destination amid a zombie outbreak of crazed straights. I guess I'd hoped for that old classic of lying in bed, surrounded by your family members as they hold your hand and tell you how much they love you.

Still, that kind of pleasant little wrap up is always a bit of wishful thinking. You never know what's gonna come out of nowhere and turn things on their head, whether that's a drunk driver or a terminal illness or a zombie attack.

At least I've got an interesting story, and that's something to be thankful for, but it's not nearly enough to quell the rage that's bubbling up inside me.

Now that I won't have to live with myself much longer, I guess I can finally admit that maybe this ire and frustration have been lurking for a while. Maybe it's been simmering since the first time I was told that I wasn't *really* bisexual because I'd only kissed a girl at that point. Maybe it's been simmering since Jason was asked to leave a restaurant for holding hands on a date. Maybe it's been simmering since someone insisted Nora was just going through a phase, and told Hazel she didn't really understand who she was.

Maybe I've been livid this whole time, and now I've finally given myself permission to feel it.

As the stars above me fade to black, I hear a low rumble, the call of angelic trumpets rolling across the desert like thunder. Out of the blackness emerges a brilliant light, but as it grows closer it gradually splits into two distinct orbs of yellowish white.

The orbs are speeding up as they rush toward me, illuminating the cowboy from behind and causing him to whip around in surprise.

Suddenly, the car horn blares, not in warning, but out of that same rage I'd finally come to terms with at the depths of my soul. The cavalry has arrived, not in the form of some half-hearted straight ally, but with Hazel and Nora behind the wheel of a mighty automobile that's barreling down some fake-ass Americana main street.

The vehicle doesn't slow down as it plows through the cowboy, his body slamming against the hood with a sickening thump and then flipping through the air like a ragdoll of shattered bones. The car doesn't stop there, continuing onward and crashing through one of the gallows posts.

The whole structure gives way under the force of this powerful machine, wood shattering and splinters erupting as the vehicle keeps pushing onward. I feel the rope instantly go slack as I drop through the hole, air flooding my lungs with a single, powerful draw. A long, deep creak emits from the collapsing platform as the whole thing begins to tip, and with my last crumbs of energy I pull the rope from my neck and frantically crawl away from the rupturing wood.

The vehicle finally comes to rest, axle bent and the whole front section completely destroyed. Smoke rises from the engine.

I struggle to my feet, anxious to check on my friends, but before I get the chance an unexpected shriek rips though the night air. My head snaps back toward Bobcat's Saloon.

Apparently, Hank's trance has been broken. I watch as the man comes sprinting out of the building, his knife held high and tears of belligerent anger streaming down his face. The two of us lock eyes as he rushes toward me, the maniac's gait transforming into a strange gallop as he smiles wide.

At this moment, I don't see a single rage-fueled zombie. I see every screaming bigot I've spared along this journey, a whole army coming at me with ruthless fire and hatred in their belly. I'm aching and exhausted, consumed by pain and frustration and, more than anything, a desire to *just be left the hell alone*. I didn't ask for any of this, none of us did.

I notice Brandon's bat lying on the ground, dropped after he took the bullet, and I reach down to pick it up. Instead of looking for ways to escape, I'm sizing up my target, taking note of the way he makes his approach.

The bartender goes to swing his knife, but I meet him head-on with a swing of my own.

Crack!

The zombie staggers back, caught off-guard by this direct hit. He attempts to collect himself, but I don't stop coming, pushing him back with strike after strike from my weapon. I'm whipping the bat back and forth, knocking his head from side to side as I gain more ground.

Words begin to spill from my mouth, one or two between every wallop. I don't think about what I'm saying, just allow the feelings to pour out of me as I release every drop of pent-up guilt that remained hidden within my body like toxic sludge.

"I'm. Not. Responsible. For. Cleaning. Up. Your. Cis. Straight. Bullshit," I cry out in a cathartic wail.

With the last strike, I send this maniac tumbling over a low wooden fence and into the old west graveyard, a fitting end for this irresponsible asshole.

I've wasted so much energy making excuses for guys like this, taken the high road so many times that I'd completely lost my sense of elevation. I hang on tight, expecting an emotional free fall after this violent outburst, but the free fall never comes.

I don't feel guilty, because none of this is my fault. I've tried my best to treat the overwhelmed with dignity, but *all of this* could've been prevented with a few basic precautions.

The reason these precautions don't happen is simple. Deep down, they just don't care enough to bother.

Suddenly, the car door falls open with a thud and Nora crawls out. Hazel follows closely after, and as the two of them stand up and dust themselves off, I'm reminded of the fact there are *some* people who care. The three of us represent vastly different personalities and stories, but together we make a community that's so much stronger than the sum of its parts.

Allies are important, of course, but tonight Brandon proved they're far from the ultimate solution. Real momentum comes when the queer community relies on each other.

Hazel, Nora and I embrace as Jason's car catches fire, orange flames bubbling up from somewhere under the crumpled hood and creeping their way into the cab. With no vehicle or gas, it looks like we're not making it to Palm Springs tonight.

The three of us hold tight, our heads pressed together as we exchange love and warmth in a completely wordless connection. We're not safe, but for a brief moment we're all happy to pretend.

The car fire grows higher and higher, and soon the prospect of remaining unseen slips away from us. We need to get moving.

We release our embrace, and right on cue, caustic howls start rumbling down the nearby hillside. Lights flicker on. The bungalows and trailers that call this little patch of land home are springing to life, announcing the folks who decided sleeping through tonight was precaution enough.

Folks who didn't care to put in the effort.

I can only imagine what's going on inside these homes, crazed straights frantically rummaging through their garage toolboxes and kitchen drawers in search of a brutal weapon. The chaos below has caught their attention, but when they sense the presence of Hazel, Nora and myself, it'll quickly become an obsession.

I glance over my shoulder at the darkness of the

open desert, feeling deeply uneasy about this escape route. While some of the overwhelmed appear to be bumbling idiots, others are more determined with their tracking skills. When hundreds of rage-fueled zombies come pouring down that hillside, we'll have nowhere to hide.

Unfortunately, we've found ourselves with limited options.

As we turn to run, we're faced with yet another gut-churning sight. While the lights of the flatlands aren't quite as numerous as their hillside counterparts, they're still out there flickering into existence.

The maniacal shrieks grow louder all around us. I can see movement under the moonlight, figures sprinting through the darkness as they're drawn by the towering flame and some supernatural knowledge of our innate queerness.

But as this cacophony of voices grows, another sound begins to fill the air.

Suddenly, a truck erupts around the bend, headlights blaring as it barrels down the highway. The vehicle slows when it approaches the fire, then kicks back into high gear when the driver's close enough to make out our three silhouettes.

The truck swerves off the road and heads toward us, throwing up a plume of dust. It skids to a stop as the driver's-side window rolls down and reveals Jason's smiling face.

"Still need a ride to Palm Springs?" he ask, the goofy delivery of this question in direct conflict with his badly bruised face and swollen eyelid.

"Oh my god," I blurt, staggering around to the

passenger side and climbing in, while Nora and Hazel dive into the back seats. "You're alive."

I slam the door behind me and throw my arms around Jason.

"Where the hell did you find this truck?" I question.

"It's Brandon's," Jason replies, then motions toward two hanging wires below the steering wheel. "Thank god it's old enough for this to work."

"Guys! Guys!" Nora suddenly interjects, grabbing our attention and pointing to a cascade of figures sprinting toward us. "Let's talk on the road."

Jason slams the gas and takes off once again, swerving onto the concrete and zooming back the way he came. I glance over my shoulder as the overwhelmed pour onto the road, chainsaws, crowbars and hammers hoisted above their heads in a state of belligerent rage.

"What happened?" I finally question, still reeling from Jason's presence.

"Fell down a hill, crawled under a rock," he explains. "The ones who get close to you can track you pretty well, so I thought I was a goner, but my phone was still connected to the drone."

Jason holds up his smartwatch. "Started up some YMCA. It was just enough time to get Brandon's ride unhooked from the tow truck and fire it up."

Nora chimes in from the back, addressing the whole car. "Uh, can they drive after us?"

"Some of them probably can," Hazel offers. "If driving was a big part of their life. I don't think their current mental facilities are going to let them drive *well.*"

STRAIGHT

I close my eyes and sink back into my chair as the vehicle rumbles below me, finally accepting that we've found a moment of relative safety. It's still a long time before Saturation Day is over, but with a full tank of gas and Palm Springs on the horizon, I'm feeling pretty good.

For a brief moment, my thoughts drift back to the attacker I'd beaten as he rushed me with that knife, but the guilt still doesn't come. I'm no longer willing to bend over backward for this unprovoked violence, no longer willing to take responsibly for the consequences of *their* fury when it invades my space and threatens my life. I will help the overwhelmed when I can, and I will live with love and mercy in my heart, but don't come at me as a screaming, rage-filled zombie and expect to be babysat.

Not any longer.

We don't travel far before noticing a lone figure on the side of the road, clutching their shoulder and staggering along. The truck slows as I sit up in my chair, amazed by what I'm seeing.

It's Brandon, wounded and barely conscious as he pushes onward through the desert. A long trail of blood spots the asphalt behind him, and without a little help I doubt he'll last much longer.

"That asshole left me to die," is all I can think to say.

While Jason has no idea what I'm talking about, Hazel and Nora are well aware. The three of us exchange glances in the rearview mirror, all thinking the same thing.

Since our first moment of conflict back at the cabin, Brandon has proven himself to be a complete prick, careless and crass in a situation that was life or death for the rest of us, but some huge joke to him.

Still, are a few obnoxious character flaws enough to turn our back on someone who clearly needs our help?

Unfortunately for Brandon, that's precisely what he did when I was strung up on the gallows. It's easy to be an ally when everything's sunny and bright, when you've got no skin in the game, but true colors always show when your back is to the ropes and the danger is right there, staring you in the face.

Jason slows the truck to a crawl, and at this point I'd expect any one of us to call out for him to keep going, leaving Brandon to die just like he'd left me.

But I say nothing.

Brandon doesn't look after his allies, but his allies are better than that. He's a lucky man, not because I've forgiven him, but because I was nothing like him in the first place.

The truck comes rolling to a full stop, causing Brandon to finally glance over at us. He's completely out of it, his face pale and his eyes weary. Our gaze meets as the windows roll down.

"You left me hanging," I call over, not quite sure what I'm expecting in return.

Brandon just stares at me for a long while. "That was your problem, not mine," he finally replies.

I let out a knowing sigh, then motion for him to get in the back seat. Nora and Hazel slide over to make room as Brandon opens the door.

Without warning, a figure lurches through the darkness and slams Brandon against the open door with so much force it bends backwards on its hinges. A battery-powered saw roars to life as the artist screams wildly, slicing Brandon right up the middle and causing his innards to spill forth in a slippery, spurting mess of red and pink.

The whole truck screams in unison as Jason slams on the gas, propelling us onward while Brandon and the artist tumble to the ground.

"There's blood on me!" Nora screams frantically. "Was I bit? Oh my God, am I gonna turn straight?"

"That's… not how it works," Hazel assures her, taking off her jacket and helping to wipe away the crimson splatter.

I take one glance back as we continue onward, watching as the artist straddles the body of his lifeless prey. He begins to saw, immediately getting to work on the next masterpiece.

They disappear into the black void behind us.

As I settle in again, I think to ask Jason if we should slow down a bit, turning off our high beams and crawling through the desert unnoticed. As this question washes through my mind, however, I quickly arrive at the answer.

We may be on the run, but we're sick to death of hiding.

The drive from Joshua Tree to Palm Springs is a little under an hour, and for the first half of this journey nobody says a word, lost in our thoughts just like we were on the way here. The blood covering the inside of Nora's door has started to darken and dry, a reminder of the past as we push onward.

"This is the longest I've seen you go without making a joke," I finally offer, breaking through the silence as my eyes flicker back to Nora.

She says nothing, the expression on her face remaining utterly static. I suppose everyone has their limits. While Nora is often a spark of joy in the most uncomfortable moments of darkness, it appears something within her has finally succumbed to the pressure of this hellish night.

Witnessing a power saw disembowelment from just a few feet away tends to do that.

More silence fills the truck.

"So *this* is straight culture," Hazel finally offers, remaining stone-faced as long as possible before finally cracking a smile.

Soon enough, I'm laughing uncontrollably with the rest of the gang.

While dubious in its appropriateness, this moment is exactly what we needed. Sometimes a little laughter is just what it takes to push through the hard stuff.

We finally crest a hill to reveal the sprawling lights of Palm Springs below. I've visited this city plenty of times, but never before have I been so moved by its glorious arrival. Our destination radiates across the desert around it like some brilliant luminescent oasis, coaxing us onward to salvation.

The closer we draw, the more I can make out new construction sprouting up around the urban limits, creating a distinct divide between the open plains and paradise beyond. A huge towering wall of metal protects the innermost layer, and several rings of protective chain-link fencing work their way outward from there.

A huge main gate rises to greet us, the only way in

or out for the evening. It's surrounded by a massive brigade of military vehicles, pride-flag insignias welded to their side.

As our truck slows even more details are revealed. The towering city walls have soldiers patrolling back and forth across them, automatic weapons at the ready. In the spaces that separate each section of fencing, a few of the overwhelmed have slipped through or climbed over, but they appear to be seriously wounded rather than deceased.

This appears to be intentional.

"Oh fuck, oh fuck, oh fuck," Jason starts repeating under his breath, growing progressively more nervous by the second.

I shoot him a confused glance. This is a moment of elation, and while I fully expect to be turned away, it's still the closest we've been to salvation thus far.

"It's gonna be okay," I offer calmly. "They might let us in. If not, maybe they'll tell us somewhere safe to go."

"That's exactly what I'm worried about," Jason counters. *"Letting us in."*

Nora can't help but scoff loudly from the backseat. "What the fuck are you even saying?"

"Have you seen *any* zombie movies?" he continues. "This is the third act, where the survivors finally make it back to what's left of civilization."

"I could use a little civilization right now, there's still blood on me," Nora retorts.

"But it *never ends there,*" Jason blurts, his anxiety peaking as we draw even closer to this looming main gate. "This is where they realize *humans* are the real monsters, not zombies. Civilization is even more fucked up."

It's been a long night, and Jason's little diatribe is

proof of that. Still, I can't help letting his words crawl under my skin a bit. Who knows what lies beyond these city walls?

Eventually, we roll to a stop. We're quickly approached by a man in a green camouflage jumpsuit, the colorful pride patch affixed to his shoulder.

Jason rolls down his window.

"Happy Saturation Day," the man in uniform offers. "Looks like you folks have had quite the night so far."

The guard pauses a moment, giving us time to respond and then continuing onward when nobody can muster the appropriate words. His expression drops, abruptly becoming more serious as he peers into the vehicle. The soldier points a flashlight directly into our faces, looking us over one by one.

Nora covers her eyes, but the guard quickly interjects. "Ma'am, I know it's uncomfortable, but please don't do that."

Finally, Nora drops her hand and stares directly into the light.

"You feeling okay?" the soldier questions.

Nora nods. "Yeah."

The man in uniform holds this position for an excruciatingly long time, then finally lowers his flashlight and turns it off.

"Everyone in the truck queer?" he asks. "Security protocol orange ended this morning. No straights in or out."

"We are," Jason replies firmly.

The guard nods. "Alright. Let's see your tickets."

Jason just stares at him, hesitating a moment before

revealing the truth of the matter. "We don't have any," he replies. "We're escaping from Joshua Tree."

All citizens of Palm Springs are welcome within the city walls on Saturation Day, these immaculate security precautions paid for by a yearly tax. Cis straight people are allowed to remain after taking a vigorous series of precautions, and outsiders are allowed inside for a hefty sum.

None of us could afford it.

The guard frowns, nodding quietly as he assesses the situation. He takes a deep breath, then calls back to a heavily armed man in the booth behind him. "Hey Peterson!"

My heart slams hard within my chest as my fingers instinctively grip the seat below me. The man in the booth appears to ready his weapon.

"Yes sir?" Peterson calls back.

The whole world stops.

"Open the gates for these folks," the original guard finally commands.

My body immediately relaxes, sinking back into my seat.

"We're all in this together, right?" the man in uniform offers. "We'll make room. Head on in."

Everyone in the vehicle watches in stunned silence as the gates open, all four layers of chain-link protection that lead us to a metal wall beyond. We putter forward, watching as the final gate opens wide and reveals a lush, tropical oasis.

Everything in Palm Springs is lit and glowing, trees wrapped in colorful neon rope and safety floodlights positioned down every dark alley. The streets are crowded with people chatting excitedly, holding beverages and hoisting them to greet our arrival.

You couldn't hear it from the outside, but now that the doors have been thrown wide open, I pick up on the thunderous rhythm of dance music rolling across the rooftops from some distant stage.

"I understand the worry," I offer Jason, my eyes darting across the gay utopia that unfolds before us, "but I can think of one big difference between those other zombie stories and this one."

***

As Hazel collapses into the chair across from us, I can't help but smile. She's wearing dark sunglasses and a hooded sweatshirt, low-key apparel I could've never imagined her sporting until this very moment.

"Something tells me you weren't buried in a book last night," I offer with a laugh.

Hazel shakes her head as Nora flops into the chair next to her, equally disheveled and hungover. "Oh, she was buried in *something* last night," Nora offers.

I reach for the Mimosa pitcher at the center of our table. They both nod without saying a word and I fill their glasses.

It's late in the morning, and Palm Springs is in chaos. Of course, it's not the same chaos the rest of the world is currently experiencing—just a really bad hangover after a long night of partying.

I lean back into my chair and take a slow, satisfying

drink, enjoying the peaceful chirp of local birds as they flirtatiously dance from one tropical perch to the next.

We're on the outdoor patio of a favorite Palm Springs restaurant. On the wall nearby, a television hangs, and in most other circumstances I'd be glued to the news, but not right now.

All the TVs and radios are turned off, at least until this year's Saturation Day is over. That's when the real frustration begins, swarms of twenty-four-hour killers turned back to their natural state and claiming everything went just fine last night.

None of them will remember a thing, but it couldn't have been that bad, *could it?*

I take another drink, this one a little longer than the first.

A waiter approaches, dropping off a small plate before each of us. A warm cookie sits at the center of each one, the delicious scent immediately filling my nostrils.

"Breakfast cookies. Compliments of the chef," he announces.

"Wait, why?" I blurt, immediately skeptical.

"Looks like you could use them," the waiter replies.

I glance around the table and swiftly recognize that, not only are we hungover, we're battered, bruised and beaten to hell.

I motion for of the waiter to come in closer. "Who made these?" I ask him under my breath as my friends dive in, wolfing their baked goods down without hesitation.

The waiter motions toward a sweet older woman in the open kitchen, cheerfully going about her business. "She makes them every morning."

I hold the man's gaze, waiting for a little more information.

"She's straight," he finally continues. "Citizens of Palm Springs are very careful."

I nod as the waiter leaves. When I turn back to my friends they're all staring at me awkwardly, unsure what the problem is.

"If you don't wanna eat that, I'll take it," Nora offers.

I gaze down at the cookie, scrutinizing it like the door of some frightening crypt or a gateway into my darkest nightmares. I can't help thinking of my neighbor, Margot, recalling the kind dessert of needles and pins she'd offered up just yesterday morning.

After finding myself literally hung out to dry, I'm having a lot of trouble gathering any kind of trust for the people who, in their own small ways, allowed this to happen.

I glance back at the woman in the kitchen once more. She's smiling and laughing with her friends, completely unaware of the fear and anxiety her offer of kindness has caused me.

Maybe I wouldn't let her watch my back during a violent confrontation in the zombie apocalypse, but that level of trust takes time.

My gaze returns to the cookie as I breathe deep and pick it up. I shoot one last look at my friends, checking for any signs of sickness or poisoning, then take a huge bite of the gooey, chocolate-chip-and-raisin-covered circle.

I chew slowly, then swallow as the sweet, buttery flavor overwhelms my taste buds. I find myself trying to be critical, to find something wrong with the mixture of glorious tangs that roll together in my mouth, but I just can't.

I swallow. "It's…complicated," I finally announce.

Jason flashes me a look of confusion. "The cookie?"

"No. Everything," I admit.

"Well, how's the cookie?" he scoffs, rolling his eyes.

I take another bite.

I'm still holding back, still just as heated and upset as I deserve to be, but the longer I carry these heavy emotions, the more I realize I'm only depriving *myself* of some very important moments. It's valid to feel anger, that much I've learned, but it's also just as valid to feel joy.

There are things to fight to the death for, and there are things to let go. There are places to take a stand, and places to find compromise.

At least when it comes to breakfast cookies.

"Alright, fine," I announce, a smile working its way across my face as I swallow the second bite and truly allow myself to enjoy it. "It's pretty fucking good."

Glancing around at my group of friends, I realize there's a side of them I got to know this weekend that I'd never seen before, an intricate balance that makes them the beautiful, complex queers I love.

None of us would've survived if it wasn't for these complexities, not just within ourselves, but as a group. We may hail from across the vast spectrum of sexualities, but we're stronger together. I now know our survival is not predicated on the conditional help of fair-weathered allies, or even the rock-solid kindness of outsiders who put in the work.

We've made it this far because of each other.

ABOUT THE AUTHOR

Chuck Tingle is a mysterious force of energy behind sunglasses and a pink mask. He is also an anonymous author of romance, horror, and fantasy. Chuck was born in Home of Truth, Utah, and now splits time between Billings, Montana and Los Angeles, California. Chuck writes to prove love is real, because love is the most important tool we have when resisting the endless cosmic void. Not everything people say about Chuck is true, but the important parts are.

Milton Keynes UK
Ingram Content Group UK Ltd.
UKHW022303250724
1024UKWH00016B/392